THE PARTNERS

THE PARTNERS

ROBERT H. REDDING

DOUBLEDAY & COMPANY, INC.
GARDEN CITY, NEW YORK
1981

Library of Congress Cataloging in Publication Data

Redding, Robert H
The partners.

(DD western)
I. Title.
PS3568.E336P37   813'.54

First Edition

ISBN: 0-385-17007-6
Library of Congress Catalog Card Number 80-1660
Copyright © 1981 by Robert H. Redding
All Rights Reserved
Printed in the United States of America

THE PARTNERS

CHAPTER 1

Tim Meeker reined his sorrel to a stop. The yellow lamps of Central cast long shadows in the spruce forest. The village was still a quarter of a mile away, but Meeker was taking no chances. He dismounted and led the way on foot.

"We got to see if the enemy is there, Buck," he whispered. "And if he is, we got to make other plans."

Though the hands on Tim's watch registered midnight, it was still just light enough to make out the trail. Tim thanked the gods for that. He hadn't been to Central in over a year, and the trail changed every spring with washouts. He picked his way carefully, avoiding mudholes. He tapped his holster and was fortified in knowing the .44 was ready. A rifle would have been better, but time telescoped so fast, there hadn't been a chance to find a heavier weapon.

Meeker grinned, despite the fatigue that dragged his bones. Who would have thought something like this of him? Timothy Meeker—"Meeky" the kids had called him in school, because he would back away from a fight if he possibly could. He didn't like fighting. And now—this!

Dogs barked, sending raucous waves through the silent forest. Tim reckoned they were either Riley's huskies or they belonged to Hansen, the mailman. If they belonged to Hansen, he had a word for him: the trail was nearly bare of snow all the way to Fairbanks. The last three days had been hot, and the white stuff had drained off the hills in rivers. The mud was two feet deep in places, and Buck was worn out, to say nothing of himself.

Tim's mind rushed ahead to Riley's roadhouse, his destination. At Riley's he would get a nice clean bed, a hot meal, and sleep, lots and lots of s-l-e-e-p! He hadn't closed his eyes for three days.

A sudden thought stopped Meeker. Could the dogs belong to a marshal, perchance? Maybe a deputy from Circle City? He had traveled fast, covering a hundred and thirty miles in three days, but a telegram took only minutes. Tim frowned and tapped his holster again. *Damn!*

An owl hooted spookily, and the forest gave it back in a faint *whoooo—whoooo!*

"It's just me, dang you!" growled Tim nervously. "Don't wake up the dead!"

He was within a couple of hundred yards of Riley's now. The square log building was shadowy in the dim light, seeming unreal and slightly fantastic—like a dragon waiting. Tim shivered. It was chilly, the May night still drew ice to quiet waters, but Tim admitted his shiver was not altogether due to the cold. He was tense as a banjo string. He didn't want to go to jail. Not one bit of it!

He led Buck into the forest a few yards and looped the reins around a tree. It would be best if he reconnoitered alone. Horsehoofs had a way of clopping in the boggy soil.

Swiftly, he closed in on the roadhouse, crouching to make his six-foot silhouette less visible. A quick look through the windows would tell all he needed to know. Old friend Riley would be there, and possibly the mailman, Hansen. All right. He knew Hansen by sight, but if there was a strange face in the big front room, it was time for caution. It might belong to the law.

He reached the wall of the roadhouse, and straightened up. As he did so, the question that had been haunting him for three days arose again. Why was *he* following the outlaw life and not Mike Garrett? Garrett was the bad guy in this, damn it all! How come, then, it wasn't Garrett shivering here, instead of himself? And how could he have been so wrong about a man!

My God, he'd known Garrett since school days in Juneau. That was a long time. Couldn't he judge character any better than that?

Tim shook his head to clear his mind and pressed an ear to the walls. He heard nothing through the ten-inch logs and started for a window, then abruptly changed his plans. The windows were chancy. The men inside were tuned to sudden changes in their surroundings. They were woodswise, noting differences rather than the familiar. Even a quick glimpse could draw their attention the same as a bolt of lightning. It would be best to go in the back shed and listen. He could hear better through the door, and as much could be learned by listening as looking.

He reached the rear, swung the shed door open silently, and then froze. Waiting there was a man with a shiny, nickel-plated badge reading U.S. DEPUTY MARSHAL pinned over his heart.

"Howdy," said the man conversationally, "I'm Dwyer, and I been waiting. Seen you up the trail quite a spell ago. What's been keeping you?"

Tim gaped.

"Give me your pistol, please," came the request.

"No," said Tim.

"Now don't make it hard on both of us, young feller."

As he spoke the deputy drew his own revolver, a .45 Colt.

Suddenly Tim lashed out with his fist and the deputy tumbled back. Tim ran. He ran as fast as he could through the tangled forest. He felt like he was in a remembered dream, in which he was running frantically but not gaining an inch.

The deputy was close behind, and he yelled, "Stop, or I'll have to shoot!"

It was then that Tim recalled his own weapon. He went for it and fired into the air, hoping his pursuer would duck and give him more of a lead. But the ruse didn't work. The brush crackled behind, and the crackles were getting closer.

Tim had a decision to make: did he want to kill a man? He

had already been accused of arson, and of busting Garrett's jaw
—did he want murder added to the list?

The answer was a quick no. He couldn't kill anybody, but he
fired the pistol again, still hoping the trick would give him time.
If he could reach Buck . . .

There was a roar behind him, and tree limbs snapped over-
head, clipped by a heavy lead slug.

"Next time, it will be you!" came the warning. "And I can't
miss. Your silhouette is like a light for me. You're a sitting
duck, Meeker. Give 'er up!"

But Tim wasn't about to "give 'er up." He faced a term in
prison unless he could prove Mike Garrett was a crook. And
how could he do that in jail? All the evidence was stacked in
favor of Mike, who had the town's ear. Mike the upstanding
citizen and philanthropist. Tim groaned in disgust.

Another shot roared, but Tim didn't hear it. He was loping
ahead full tilt one moment, and then he wasn't running any
more at all. He crashed into a heap of waterlogged snow and
lay still. Blood from a crease along his right temple turned the
snow crimson.

The deputy puffed up alongside of his target and swore,
"Damn it, man! I *ast* you to stop. Damn it all, anyways!"

When Tim regained consciousness, his head was wrapped in
a bandage, and he lay flat on a bunk in the roadhouse. Riley's
wrinkled visage hovered anxiously over his.

"Huh," grunted the old man. "You all right, Timmy? Had
me goin' there for a while, son."

The Circle City deputy marshal stepped into view. He was a
stocky man, with a beefy red face and watery light-blue eyes.

"Why in hell did you run?" he demanded angrily. "You
knew I'd have to shoot!"

Tim raised himself up, then dropped back, his senses spinning. He shut his eyes against the whirling room.

He heard the deputy ask Riley, "Is it going to be okay to
cart him back to Circle?"

"Sure, Dwyer, sure!" was Riley's testy affirmation. "But you come awful close to killin' this man. Half an inch over, you wouldn't have to worry about takin' him nowheres!"

"The thing I can't understand," said Dwyer, "is why he didn't plug me. He could have done it easy. Just stopped and took aim. Hell."

"This boy is no killer" was the salty rejoinder. "I know him, and I knew his daddy and he was a fine man. I don't know what Tim Meeker done to deserve the attention of the law, but I'll vouch he ain't guilty of it." Riley's voice went up a notch. "Is he?"

"How do I know? All's I know is that he's in trouble, and I got orders to bring him in. Seems like he set a fire."

"Bull-oney!" argued Riley. "You ought to go easy, Dwyer. After all, he didn't blast you. That ought to be worth somethin'!"

"But he did fire two shots," countered Dwyer, "you heard the forty-four, Riley. It sounds different than my forty-five. I don't see how he missed."

While this conversation was rumbling back and forth over his head, Tim's addled brain gradually regained stability. He spoke up.

"I fired in the air to scare you, was all."

The deputy nodded.

"Maybe I believe you," he said. "Anyways, that's how I'll tell it in court."

"But you will tell?"

"I got to tell it like it is, young feller. An' if the judge believes that's what you done, he'll go lighter, maybe."

"That 'maybe' is what scares me," muttered Tim. "I could get more jail time if he don't believe it." Things were getting much worse. Tim sighed heavily. "Think he'll believe me?"

"Yeah," said Dwyer, but the word came out loaded with skepticism.

Tim noted that the sun was spreading a yellow curtain over the log ceiling. He sat upright. His head went spinning again, but he clutched the bunk and remained sitting.

"What time is it?" he asked the room.

"Ten in the ay-em," responded Riley. "You got the hungrys, maybe?"

"I got a horse tied out there," said Tim. "The poor devil's probably cold and starved."

"Naw," replied the roadhouse proprietor, "Hansen took off early, while the trail still had overnight frost crust. He found the critter and brought him back. We figured he was yours."

"We got to get going," interrupted Dwyer. "It's thirty mile to Circle and I want to be there by dark."

Tim made no response to this. His mind was a despairing bog. The only thing he was really guilty of in this whole sad affair was letting loose the two shots. All the rest could be laid to his partner, Mike Garrett. If it was true he had busted Mike's jaw, like Lindstrum said, it was done in a fair and square fight. As far as he was concerned, there was no guilt in that. It might be true that he had caused the fire, but, hell, that was during the fight, too, and he'd accidentally knocked over a kerosene lamp. That could happen to anybody, but Mike was crying arson!

Riley had disappeared into the kitchen, and soon after the delicious odor of bacon and eggs and hot coffee drifted through the building. Dwyer sat near Tim, unmoving, his watery eyes alert, like those of a hunting falcon.

Tim swung his feet to the floor. Though his head still gave trouble, the floor remained level when he stood up.

"Where are you goin'?" demanded the deputy.

"Where does anybody go after a night's sleep?" Tim shot back.

"Well, I got to come with you," growled Dwyer. "We are pals now, young feller. We are in-sep-ar-ate-able, understand? You are very valuable to me."

"Valuable?"

"Yeah. Garrett has offered three thousand in cash to anybody who brings you in. An' that includes lawmen!"

CHAPTER 2

It was 11 A.M. before the two hit the trail. The deputy forked a black gelding, and followed Tim astride Buck. Buck had rested and was full of oats, kindness of Riley.

The two-man procession single-filed through the forest, to the rhythm of hoofs thudding on the melted earth. The spruce, stunted gargoyles of the Alaskan taiga, seemed hostile to Tim. Why can't you be birch trees, he thought, they are so much more *friendly!*

A mournful dogs' chorus kept pace for a while, which didn't help Tim's spirits. Riley had eleven huskies, though he didn't use them much anymore. Old age and lumbago prohibited long trips. Trapping days were finished, and he made a living from the roadhouse, which he built himself. But he kept the dogs, along with a couple of horses.

"I just can't give those critters away," he declared at breakfast, "or shoot 'em, for cri' sakes! They been my friends for years, and they'll live till they die natural like."

And so the dogs spent their lives howling, eating, sleeping, and from time to time breaking loose to romp in the forest, giving Riley fits until he found them again.

There were times when Tim enjoyed a howl. Most of the huskies were of mixed blood, which meant a quart or so of wolf corpuscles, as well as malamute and Siberian. The wolf strain made nice music, but today Tim's nerves shrieked. He was glad when the horses finally plodded out of earshot.

An Alaskan jay fluttered ahead and lit on one of the glowering spruce. The bird's black eyes took in the two men. Did they have something to eat? He cooed softly, then broke into a rash squawking. Moments later, another jay partnered up with him, and the two followed along, alternately cooing and cackling.

"Nothing for you guys yet," Tim warned. "We don't eat for a long time."

"How's that?" called Dwyer from the rear.

"I was just talking to a couple of camp robbers," explained Tim. "Have you got anything for them?"

Dwyer apparently didn't think that was worth answering, and the silence behind thickened.

Lucky birds, thought Tim. All they have to worry about is their next meal. I wonder if they know how much freedom they have?

"What do you expect will happen?" he called over his shoulder.

"Oh, they can find something someplace!" came a grumpy reply.

"No—I don't mean those birds, I mean about *me!*"

"You?"

"Yeah. Will I stay in the Circle calaboose long?"

"I don't know, pardner." Dwyer was feeling mean. "Maybe they'll keep you locked up till the first riverboat comes in. That ought to be the end of this month. Then they'll send you to Fairbanks on it. Or maybe they'll send you back over the trail. Hell, I don't know." There was a pause, then Dwyer added shortly, "And maybe they'll hang you right now! Circle ain't had any excitement since the Jewell brothers busted up the Pioneer Saloon three weeks back."

"Thanks a lot," muttered Tim.

He knew his offense—alleged offense—wasn't a hanging matter, but Dwyer needn't be quite so grim about it.

Tim thought about Ruth, and a bitter smile turned his pleasant face hard. There she had been, cozied up to Garrett, real chummy, talking mouth to mouth almost. There was something in the way she presented herself to his partner—erstwhile partner?—that had turned his blood to molten fire. He, Tim Meeker, who had dodged fights all his life, saw red in that moment.

Perhaps he should have let it go. Maybe he shouldn't have stalked into the Aurora, maybe he shouldn't have stiff-legged to the table and sat down with them. None of this would have come to pass, if he hadn't done that!

On the other hand, maybe it would. It may have been only a matter of time before his conscience wouldn't take no for an answer. He'd never really be sure of that now, but he granted himself the possibility.

He had known for some time that Garrett was selling illegal bootleg, passing it off as the real McCoy to customers. But when he objected, Garrett overrode him with, "Hell, those creek bears don't care what they drink! They're fresh off the mines with gold and they want to spend it!"

Tim felt a little abashed under Garrett's cold eye, but he said, "A lot of that stuff is poison, Mike. Anything goes wrong, and you—we, actually—could land in jail."

Mike Garrett was a big man, over six feet tall, heavy as a hogshead of flour—outweighing Tim by a hundred pounds. He feared nobody and had the scars to prove it. He was particularly proud of a thick, handlebar moustache that covered his upper lip like a black bowie knife.

He twirled his pride and joy and grinned evilly, saying, "Meeky, nothing will happen. Don't fret your timid soul about it! I know the right people in this camp, and they like what I give 'em."

"You mean you're bribing the law?"

"I'll never tell, sonny."

"Why not? I'm equal partners and have a right to know what goes on."

"Just keep smiling, Tim boy. I'll do the rest."

Garrett had always been patronizing. Though they were the same age, Garrett acted older, and, brainwise, he *was* older. He was clever and could see things that were vague to Tim. They had gone to Juneau schools together and had come north shortly after the little Italian Felix Pedro made his bonanza strike. It was a strike that changed a wilderness into a thriving mining town within a year. The two had some money, and they opened the Aurora Tavern on equal shares.

From the start, the saloon was a money-maker. Though the big discoveries of Pedro and others, like Tom Gilmore and the Berry brothers, were recent history, the creeks for fifty miles around were gold rich, too. Eldorado, Vault, Dome and a dozen more were being mined by small operators. Small or not, they were all making money. The Fairbanks mining district was wealthy!

Tim had backed down from his objections to Garrett's bootleg. Maybe it wasn't so bad, he told himself. Most of the bars were selling it, so it must not be all wrong. And it was probably true the miners didn't care what they drank. After seven days of twelve-hour shifts, they were loaded for bear and didn't come to town looking for mice. They didn't quibble. They wanted a quick jolt of fun and forgetfulness, and bootleg was just as efficient at that as the legal stuff.

But, then, he'd stumbled onto something else. Garrett was drugging the drinks of customers who were especially affluent. When they passed out, Sike Hendrickson, one of Garrett's boys, lifted the man's poke, and then saw to it the unconscious body was carted to a whorehouse on the Line. When the poor joker woke up, he had no idea where he'd been or what he'd done. For all he knew, he had blown his wad on women. It was a slick operation, and the girls were well paid for their part.

He and Garrett got into it good over that.

"I'll buy you out, Meeker!" Garrett had finally shouted. "If you don't like the way I fill the cashbox, then get out, sonny!"

"You'll land us all behind bars!" Tim had shouted back, knowing how futile his words would be.

Garrett then let loose one of his terrible bowie-knife grins,

and said, "If you squawk, I'll personally break your neck."
Then, in an easier tone, "Don't worry about it, Timmy. Like I
told you, I know my way around."

Tim conducted an investigation on his own. He had to see
who it was Garrett was paying off. In the end, he concluded
that the thing hadn't gone that far—yet. Garrett evidently
figured, however, that in case of trouble he could reach first
aid.

Again, Tim had backed down. He cursed himself for his
weakness, but he was afraid of Garrett. He, himself, was no
fighter, and though he was ashamed of his fear, it was there,
and he acknowledged the fact.

As if bootleg and doping weren't enough, Tim then found
that Garrett was practicing extortion on the Line's prostitutes.
The Line was a special area, set aside for prostitution. About
thirty women made their living practicing the world's oldest
profession. They were vulnerable, subject to expulsion by city
authorities if there was trouble. Garrett took advantage of their
fear and made them pay a weekly "fee" for "protection." Protection from bullyboy Sike Hendrickson.

Big Marge, a leader of the prostitute coterie, told Tim about
it.

"Hell!" she had shouted, "That big you-know-what has us
over a barrel. We yell to the cops, and they shut us down. Garrett has them all fooled!"

On top of all of that, Tim learned that Garrett ran crooked
card games. He imported sharks from Seattle and other points
south and reaped the rewards of ill-conceived diligence. The
man was getting to be another Soapy Smith, the notorious
Skagway hoodlum, who paid for his schemes with a hot .30-30
slug in his heart.

Unhappy and frustrated, Tim thought seriously about selling
out. But there was a stubbornness in him that welled up and
wouldn't let him run. He might be afraid of Garrett but damned

if he'd give in. And there *was* the money. Tim was stacking up more of it than he ever dreamed possible.

At the end of their last argument, Garrett had growled, "Let me take care of the business end, and you continue to shill."

The designation "shill" rankled, but Tim didn't call Garrett on it. In a way, Garrett was right. Their original agreement had been for him to be the greeter, the nice guy with a smile, the friendly friend. Since arriving in Fairbanks, he had come to know hundreds of men and women. His was the type of personality that drew people to him. They trusted him, and patronized the Aurora, feeling safe. His open personality brought in many customers, and even Garrett admitted it was a decided asset.

Yet here he was allowing bootleg and the drugging of customers—not to mention crooked card games, and extortion! In the eyes of the law, Tim knew he'd be as guilty of these crimes as his partner, even though he never took a part in them. Tim hated himself, wallowed in indecision, and let the matter go on. In the process, he became something less than a man in his own eyes.

Even so, he might have done nothing had it not been for Ruth. When he saw her with Garrett that evening, an explosion went *bang!* in his gut. The way Garrett *hunched* toward Ruth got to him. In the arrogant thrust of Garrett's shoulders, Tim read a sexual invitation that was unmistakable—and Ruth was letting it happen.

He'd met her two years before. She arrived in town with scarcely a nickel and applied for work at the Aurora, because, she said, it was so clean looking.

"I'll do anything," she said. "Wash dishes, swab, cook, bake, keep books . . ."

"We don't have work for women," Tim had told her, and she looked so disappointed that he added quickly, "Maybe you ought to try the Model Cafe. Old Tom Yule might need a waitress."

Tim had been smitten from the start. Never too bold with the girls, there was something about Ruth Claxton that put him at ease. Maybe it was her wide-set, gray eyes that did it. Eyes that brimmed with honesty and innocence. They went well with blond hair, a pert nose, and full, red lips. Under the heavy traveling clothes a lovely figure made itself unmistakably known.

"Thank you," she had answered, in a voice set to music, so far as Tim was concerned. "I'll try the Model, then."

"Perhaps I should go along," Tim had responded, to his own vast amazement. "I know Tom, and he owes me a favor."

"That would be nice" was the gracious acceptance.

She had been given a job at once, because as Yule had pointed out, "Only a fool would keep a face like that out of his place of business."

Since that day, Ruth had prospered.

It was taken for granted that she was Tim's girl. Ruth didn't seem to mind, and Tim was a happy man. He loved doing things for her, buying her clothes and jewelry. He'd given her a necklace of Cleary Creek nuggets on her twenty-second birthday and an ivory brooch set in gold just for the giving. Tim loved to see her gray eyes light up when she received presents. Once, he had three dozen long-stemmed roses shipped twenty-five hundred miles from Seattle in the dead of winter. They arrived almost fresh in a chartered sled from Valdez and were the talk of the town. Ruth was more than pleased by all the attention the roses brought. She liked the limelight, Tim observed, but so what? He gave willingly. Even the small house she occupied on First Avenue was by courtesy of himself. He had signed the deed over to her free and clear.

Ruth was an amateur painter and, so far as Tim was concerned, very talented. She loved landscapes, and Tim saw to it that she got the best views. On weekends in summer, and even on good winter days, he accompanied her to favored places so she could sketch. Her scenes of the Tanana Valley brought her a small fame, and she even sold some of her paintings. She gave Tim two of them, and he hung them in the Aurora Tavern, so all could see and enjoy. Tim was very proud of Ruth's talent, though his pride in no way reflected his true feelings. They were separate. Ruth could have been the worst artist in the world, and he'd have loved her as much.

For two years they'd "kept company." And in all that time, Tim never laid so much as a lustful finger on her, never a hint. They kissed gently, held hands, promenaded arm in arm through the town's main streets on Sunday, but nothing else was ever brought up. Ruth, Tim was convinced, was a "good girl," the kind who would think about "it" only after the wedding took place.

For two years he had been a happy man, proud because, to him, Ruth was easily the most beautiful woman in town, and she was his. Such a thing had never happened to him before, not to Timid Meeky, the guy who never dated simply because he was too bashful to ask. He planned to marry Ruth. Just the thought of it sent such a thrill into his heart as to leave him weak.

And then four nights ago—*only four?* it seemed like eons—he had seen her with Mike Garrett. As he had approached the table, he knew it was over between him and Ruth. The very currents of the smoky room between them carried the news like an electric shock.

Nevertheless, he asked pleasantly (always pleasant!), "Ruth, what brings you here?"

"Don't bother us, sonny," Garrett threw in. "This is between Ruth and me."

Tim ignored the remark. He took Ruth's arm, saying, "You don't want to stay here. Let me take you home."

But Ruth had snatched her arm free and stood next to Garrett.

"I want to stay, Tim," she had replied in that musical voice. "Mike and I are talking business."

"You don't want to do business with him," Tim went on. "He's a crook. You don't belong with him."

"Don't say that!" was the sharp retort.

"He sells bootleg and robs his customers," Tim proceeded doggedly, though his voice was as tight as wire rope.

That was when Garrett had slugged him. The fist came up from the floor and hit with a loud, cracking noise that turned all heads.

The blow did something that Garrett hadn't intended. It blasted all the fear out of Tim. Though he was sent crashing to the floor, he sprang up like a cornered lynx and charged into his partner. They toppled to the floor kicking, clawing, pummeling, nothing barred.

Mike bucked out from under Tim and scrambled to his feet. Tim was on him like a wild man. They stood toe to toe, trading punches until, suddenly, Tim saw flashes and bright lights and then was swallowed by a black void.

When he came to, he was in Jake Lindstrum's cabin. Jake, another friend from Juneau, was washing his face with a warm cloth. The cloth was pink with diluted blood.

"By God," said Jake, "she really whacked you."

"She?"

"Uh-huh. Ruth. She hit you with a bottle."

"*Ruth?*"

"Yeah." Jake poured a tall drink of bourbon in a tumbler. "Drink this. It'll help."

Tim gulped the whiskey.

"Are you sure it was Ruth who hit me?"

"I saw her, my friend. I had just come in, and I saw her swing from behind you."

Jake winced.

"I figured she'd killed you, man."

Tim got up and slung on his mackinaw.

"Where are you going?" demanded Jake.

"Back to the Aurora. I got to find Ruth."

"You won't find her there."

"Why not? Seems she's at home in the place."

"You won't find her there," Jake repeated, "because the place caught fire."

Tim stared.

"Yeah," said Jake. "Hell, I'm sorry to be bringing all this great news to you, but it's true. When she hit you, you crashed into a kerosene lamp, and it tipped over. There was fire everywhere. The whole place was hot as hell."

"Good grief!"

Tim corralled his scattered thoughts with an effort. After a dismal job of it, he asked, "You say I caused the fire?"

"Well, that's what I heard Garrett tell Tod Cowles."

Cowles was a district deputy marshal, a good and fair man, as far as Tim knew.

"That's only Garrett's story," protested Tim. "Cowles will want more evidence than that."

"He's got witnesses," Jake pointed out. "There's Sike Hendrickson, for example . . ."

"But Sike wasn't there . . ."

"Do you think that will make any difference? Then there's . . ." Jake hesitated.

"Ruth?"

"Yeah. And more if Garrett needs 'em."

"Well, you saw what happened!"

"Do you really think what I said would make any difference? Listen, it ain't no secret how powerful Garrett is, Tim. He could buy a dozen witnesses that would swear they saw you take and deliberately throw that lamp down. And the law couldn't do much about it."

Jake fidgeted uneasily.

"Listen," he said, "I packed you outta there in the thick of the excitement and smoke. I don't think they know where you are, but you better leave town."

"Not on your life. I'm going to set matters straight."

Jake shook his head.

"You don't get the picture," he pressed. "They are after you,

Tim. I could tell that the way Garrett was ranting." He gave
Tim a shrewd look. "You got something on him, maybe?"

"Yeah. The guy is crooked. He's worried about what I know,
all right—especially now after what happened tonight. If he
could get me thrown into jail and if I then made any holler
about his cheating ways, hell, who would believe a convict?
They'd all think it was sour grapes."

Jake poured another drink for Tim and one for himself.

"Before you and I got away from there, I heard Garrett ask
Cowles to get a warrant for your arrest. He's going to charge
you with arson and assault."

"Assault!"

Jake grinned. "You broke his jaw."

Tim felt a grim joy at this, but he was still undecided.

"He started the fight . . ."

Jake cut him off with a wave of his hand.

"Listen! Ruth says you slugged her, too. That you beat her!
And she'll swear to that, Tim. I heard her tell Cowles that you
went insane, you were uncontrollable, a mad dog, and a whole
lot more!"

Jake looked suddenly at the man staring back at him and
swore softly. "Hell, didn't you know about them?"

"Who?"

"Why, Garrett and your lady. They've been meeting behind
your back for a year. Everybody knows it. I thought you did.
She's thick with him, my friend. Real thick!"

CHAPTER 3

Tim Meeker was gloomy. It wasn't only the business of becoming an outlaw through the false assertions of others that had turned him dour. It was the loss of Ruth. He could kid about Garrett's broken jaw, but he couldn't kid about his broken heart. Until now, he'd been so busy escaping that he hadn't really had any time to feel his emotions. But now, in the lull of captivity, Jake Lindstrum's words charged into his memory like a herd of buffalo.

"They've been meeting behind your back for a year!"

That was only Jake's say, of course, but the man had no reason to lie or exaggerate. He had known Lindstrum since they were both knee high to a polar bear, and there wasn't a dishonest thought in his head. Jake was a good man, a real man. He had the reputation of being top fur-getter in the interior, no small accomplishment among the world's best. He was as open as a clear-water river. You could see all there was to Jake immediately, and if he said Ruth was "thick" with Mike, then she was.

Then why hadn't the guy come to him before? Tim shook his head at the idea. That would have not been characteristic of his friend. Jake's motto was to the point: don't butt in. He minded his own business and would even in so important a matter. Besides, had Jake told him, he probably wouldn't have believed it, and there'd have been hard feelings. Jake was smarter than people gave him credit for.

La-di-da! What a mess!

Buck tossed his head and snorted. It was a trick he had when something pleased him.

"We're coming to Birch Creek soon," Tim called back to the watchful Dwyer. "Ole Buck tells me he wants a drink. That all right?"

"Yup" was the reply.

"Is the bridge washed out?"

"Yup" came the monotone.

Talkative chap, reflected Tim, but, then, he'd said all that was essential at that.

An unbidden thought came: what were Garrett and Ruth doing now? Probably "thick." Tim's emotions took a dive when the picture of the two flashed into his mind. Damn it all! He had loved Ruth, no doubt about that. She could have had anything she wanted from him. Anything! What did Garrett have that he didn't! Brawn? Brains? Money? What in the world had it been? And why sneak around? All she had to do was tell him she preferred Mike Garrett, and he wouldn't have stood in her way. He loved her too much to have kept her, had she not been happy. He'd never stake claims on doubtful ground. Couldn't she have seen that?

There was an answer, and it wasn't a very nice one, but Tim knew it to be the only logical solution to a seemingly illogical act. Ruth was playing him for a sucker. Maybe she was playing them both for suckers—he wouldn't know—but *he* had been suckered, and there was no doubt about it. Behind those innocent gray eyes was a calculating witch.

As for Garrett? He'd come out of all this smelling like a rose. He'd open the Aurora again, no doubt of it. He knew the moneyed people in town, and the Aurora was a good risk. Garrett would get it all back—and Ruth as well!

Tim growled aloud and tried to shove his damaging thoughts away. At least there was one good thing to know: he hoped Garrett's busted jaw hurt like hell! But before Tim's morbid thoughts vanished altogether, an image of Ruth floated before the inner screens of his mind. Those lovely, honest eyes! That beautiful figure! And now Mike was probably up to his neck in both . . . my God!

Birch Creek was swollen with spring runoff. The wooden bridge was useless. Though there no longer was any ice, the damage had been done during breakup when great chunks, some of them weighing tons, smashed into the center pilings. The bridge sagged, forming a bow in the middle.

"A butterfly couldn't land tippy-toe on that thing," observed Dwyer. "We'll have to ford."

"You know a place?"

"Head downstream about a hundred yards. I crossed there two days ago and it was all right."

"How did you know I'd be coming to Central?" Tim wondered suddenly.

"I didn't" was the laconic reply. "It was a gamble. There's another deputy waiting for you at Brooks, and still another at Big Delta on the Richardson Trail."

"You covered all points, then?"

"Just about. There was Eagle, but we figured you wouldn't head there. It's a bottleneck. 'Course, you could have crossed the Yukon and got into Canada there, so we did let the Mounties know you might be along."

"What the God damn hell!" Tim ejected angrily. "My so-called crimes weren't that serious!"

"You don't call arson and burglary serious?"

"*Burglary!*"

"Sure, according to Garrett and Miss Claxton both, you took and emptied the till."

"What rot! How could I rob my own place?"

"That ain't for me to say, boy. You'll have to bring that up in court."

Tim was so mad that he clamped his jaws shut, before he began to scream nonsense. Robbery, for God's sakes!

He worked Buck downstream in a kind of numb vacuum. How Ruth must have detested him!

"Hold up!" called Dwyer. "This is the place."

The bank dropped off about a foot, directly into the current. The creek was a hundred and fifty feet wide, Tim guessed, and flowing swiftly. It had become more river than creek.

"Don't look so great to me," he advised.

"Been some more runoff," agreed Dwyer. "She's a little deeper, maybe. But this has to be it. There ain't no other crossings for two mile on either side of the bridge. Let's go!"

Tim shrugged and eased Buck over the bank. The water immediately gave battle to the horse's shanks, sending up a gurgling spray. The bottom was pure gravel, and the rounded rocks were slippery. Buck edged ahead under Tim's coaxing, going slow, testing each step. His body was tense with strain, because Buck had crossed such streams before and he knew the danger.

Deputy Dwyer followed, the black gelding nervous and jumpy. Tim could hear the man soft-talking the horse in an effort to soothe him.

The middle was deep, the water pushing high around Buck's flanks. Tim felt the heavy thrust of the current against his upside leg and did some talking himself.

"Easy, Buck old baby," he intoned gently. "Don't hurry now. You just take it nice and easy, sweetheart. All will be well, son. Trust me."

He patted Buck's neck reassuringly and scratched between the perked ears to soften the animal's rising panic. He kept up an easy chatter, encouraging the horse, urging him on, when, without warning, they stepped off into nothing.

Down they went, down, down, until Buck's flailing hoofs struck bottom and shoved them up again. Tim was still in the saddle, clinging to the pommel, as Buck lunged crazily trying to find footing. His front feet struck at the air, and he rose nearly straight up on his hind legs. All the while Tim hung on for dear life. He tensed against Buck's falling backward into the river, for he was certain that was next. But the front feet hit bottom again and Buck plowed forward, fanning water in a great spray until the mighty muscles carried them safely ashore.

Tim slid out of the saddle and looked for Dwyer. He turned just in time to see the lawman go down in the same hole.

When Dwyer came up, he was no longer on the gelding. The horse was drifting downstream. He hit a submerged boulder and tumbled end over end. All Tim could see as the animal righted itself was the head. The ears were perked, and his fear-filled eyes fastened directly on Tim. But there was nothing that could be done, and as Tim watched, the gelding sank from sight without a struggle.

In the meantime, Dwyer was swimming for shore and not doing too good a job of it. Tim knew that you didn't battle a springtime river for very long, especially when you were fully clothed. And the deputy wore a heavy sheepskin jacket over all.

"Shake off your jacket!" Tim yelled.

But Dwyer continued to pound the water with steadily weakening strokes, and Tim realized that the deputy couldn't hear him above the surface noise of the creek. Dwyer was going to drown. There was no doubt about it. Nor was there any doubt in Tim's mind as to what must be done.

He raced downstream until he was well below the struggling man. As he ran he stripped off his top clothing and boots and dove without hesitation into what he judged to be the right spot. When he came up, Dwyer was only a few feet away. He snatched the man's arm, then made for shore, stroking with his free arm.

Tim was a powerful swimmer, in spite of a skinny build. He had spent many a Juneau hour in Mendenhall Lake, diving in water refrigerated by the giant glacier of the same name. And on a visit to Wrangell he had once swum the Stikine River just after breakup, when the water was so swift that even the gas-powered mail launch clung to its dock until a more reasonable time. Water didn't frighten Tim. It was the one area where he harbored no doubt, and right now that lack of fear guided a calm mind, and that calm mind saved Deputy Marshal Dwyer's life.

Tim sunk his swimming arm deep into the current, as deep as a Tlingit Indian's paddle and they made progress. Dwyer helped with weak flips of his free hand, and the two reached shore. They were bushed and chattered with cold, but they were safe.

"Man," spluttered Dwyer, "that was close."

"I thought you said that was a good crossing," said Tim wryly.

"I must have missed that hole just by luck" was the exhausted comment. "Just by luck."

When both had regained enough strength, they returned to Buck, who was peacefully munching fresh grass. Tim donned his wet clothing, a plan forming in his mind. He mounted the sorrel and grinned down at Dwyer.

"Here," he said, "is where we part company. I'm sorry about your gelding," he added, truly meaning it, "but this is a dangerous part of the world for man and beast alike."

Dwyer reached for his .45 and found the holster empty.

"And my gun went with your horse," Tim said. "That means —it's so long for now."

The deputy shrugged.

"There ain't much I can do," he admitted. "But breaking away from me will just add to the counts against you."

Tim nodded.

"Sure it will, but listen: if I can prove that my good ole partner, Mike Garrett, has set me up and I'm innocent of everything he declares—then, all of this will count for nothing, right?"

Dwyer nodded.

"Then you better start hiking for Circle. You got fifteen miles or so to go, and by the time you get there, I'll be off—for somewhere! You'll never find me." Then, in a moment of bitterness, he added, "Hope you don't get chewed by a grizzly bear!"

Dwyer nodded again and said, "They don't scare me. And, for what it's worth, thanks for saving my life."

"I'd do as much for a dog," said Tim.

With a curt wave of his hand, he headed Buck back into the current. The horse objected at first, but he was too well trained to disobey for long and he stepped off, trembling.

Instead of going directly across, Tim played a hunch and walked Buck upstream a couple of rods before turning him toward the opposite bank. His hunch proved correct. Though the water was deep, there were no dangerous holes, and they reached shore without trouble.

Tim turned in the saddle, waved to Dwyer who was watching the operation—in hopes, thought Tim, in hopes. The deputy waved back, and Tim wasted no time. He prodded Buck into full speed toward Riley's.

The old man was surprised to see him.

"You didn't . . . ?" he asked anxiously.

"No, I didn't kill him."

Tim explained briefly, then unfolded his plan.

"Riley, I'm not guilty of anything, except busting Garrett's jaw, and he had that coming. Now listen: Jake Lindstrum told me I could use his cabin down Birch Creek, and I'm going to hide there till I get things sorted out. As far as you know, and you'll be asked, I headed lickety-split for Fairbanks. Will you tell them that?"

"Sure will, son. I owe your daddy that much."

Tim knew that back in earlier times, ten years before Felix Pedro's strike, his father and Riley had been prospecting partners. They were looking into the possibilities of the upper Porcupine, when Riley was knocked over by a brown bear. He'd have been badly mangled, probably killed, but for Tim's father, who shot the bear dead. Then the elder Meeker had boated

Riley to Fort Yukon for medical help. He was on the oars for two straight days and nights, and arrived almost dead himself, but his action had saved Riley.

"Because of your dad," Riley said once, "I've had many more years of sweet women and good whiskey, and I ain't goin' to forget it."

"I don't know just what supplies are at Lindstrum's," Tim finished. "Can you let me have a rifle and shells?"

"You can have a complete outfit," declared Riley. "Anything's mine is yours."

In an hour Tim had a pack ready. He lashed it across Buck, behind the saddle.

"I don't know when I'll see you again," he told the old man, "but don't worry. I know my way around the woods." And with considerable acid, he added, "A lot better than I do in the city!"

As Tim struck through the forest on a seldom used cross-country route to lower Birch Creek, he pondered the inscrutable machinations of fate. Five days before (or was it four?), he had been an honest citizen—well, fairly honest, anyway. He was respected, and he was in love with the most wonderful woman in creation. Never did he dream that he, one, would become an outlaw with a price on his head or, two, that he'd lose the love of his life.

CHAPTER 4

Tim felt his way through the forest, like a man in a dark room. The trail was faint, readable to Tim, only because he had followed such trails before. A pressed clump of grass, a broken willow, a scuffed patch of moss gave Tim signs that he was not wandering.

Even so, he wasn't sure. "Hell," he muttered to Buck, "for all I know we might end up in Circle."

Their way led northwest. Jake had told him the trail made contact with Birch Creek ten miles from Riley's. Because of the lay of the land, though, the bridge was fifteen. The beauty of Jake's route lay in the fact that only he used it and nobody else had followed the old river trail from the bridge in years. It was almost grown over with willows. This promised seclusion, at least for a little while, enough time to think things out. If Riley kept a poker face when the law confronted him, Jake's cabin meant a fair hideout.

After three hours, Tim reached Birch Creek. Here, his progress slowed even more, because willow and other growths threw up a jungle so thick that riding became a chore. After he'd steered Buck for a quarter of a mile, Tim felt as if he'd run an Iroquois gantlet. His face and hands stung from a hundred whips, so he dismounted and led Buck on foot. Sweaty and hot, he shouldered his way through the brush grimly. City living had softened him, and he cursed his weakness. But it was Jake's place or nothing, and he plowed on. He plowed grimly on, while time passed into the early morning of the next day.

For the hundredth time, his mind returned to Ruth. Sweet

Ruth! The girl with the wide set, honest eyes. If a man couldn't trust a woman like that, who could he trust? His heart ached, adding to his physical misery. To make matters still worse, his mind, unfettered by willows, flew away, and returned with a lurid picture of Garrett and Ruth making love.

"God!" exclaimed Tim, causing Buck to flare his nostrils. "Oh, good God!"

He tried shaking the picture from his mind, wrestling for supremacy in that dark country, but he won only half a victory. Ruth vanished, but Garrett lingered, full face, black bowie-knife moustache curled up, agreeing with the sneering lips it concealed.

"Damn you!" exploded Tim, and again Buck's nostrils flared. "You bastard! Why did you do this, Garrett? *Why?*"

He'd have gladly driven a stake through the man's heart and pulled that damned moustache out hair by hair.

Mike had always bested him. Had, somehow, always known how to manage him. Even as boys back home, Mike led, he followed. Yet, through all the years of growing up together, he'd never been given a clue as to Garrett's real character. He hadn't minded the man's arrogance, excusing it as mostly bluster. His partner was from the "other side of the tracks," as it was put, though there were no railroads in Juneau. His father had been a drunken bum, and his mother, well, she knew too much about the red-light girls on Franklin Street. Mike had had his bad times, no doubt, but did they make him such a man as to turn on a friend?

"God!" Tim yelled against the blue sky. "What a bastard he is!"

There must be a way, he thought bitterly, to show the world what Garrett really was. Great man? Philanthropist? Yes—but on what kind of money did his partner—*ex*-partner—operate?

As he shouldered his way through the barrier nature thrust at him, a tingling in his spine led Tim back to the present. Garrett's hard visage slipped behind a screen, while Tim sur-

veyed his surroundings with a shrewd eye. He'd spent much
time in the deep forests of southeastern Alaska, the Panhandle
country. There were certain signals that he'd learned to respect.
When he felt as he did now, tense without apparent reason, it
meant that instinct was working, instinct developed from prior
experience. He knew that right now a pair of eyes watched him
and Buck, or a nose had caught their scent. He couldn't be sure
who or what it was—possibly a bear. He had survived several
such encounters.

He paused and pulled a rifle from its scabbard, a .45-70
Riley lent him. It was a heavy weapon, with an octagon barrel
and a long, scarred stock.

"You can have my .30-30," the roadhouse keeper offered,
"lighter weight."

But Tim preferred the heavier gun. He took it, and a .22 rifle
for small game.

The heft of the weapon relaxed him some. He didn't like
bears. He wasn't exactly afraid of them, but became extremely
soft-footed when they were around. He'd seen the results of too
many maulings to foster any illusions that bears were noble
creatures. Men with faces half chewed off, legs mangled, arms
missing had told a different story. And he'd seen some who no
longer resembled humans at all. They fitted into burlap bags
piece by piece.

After a few more rods, he came to a clearing and stopped. It
was time for hardtack and a smoke. He was weary and hoped
Jake's cabin would turn up soon. Before eating, he led Buck to
the river and let him drink. The horse sucked in the water
gratefully, lifting his muzzle at length with a long sigh.

The queer feeling of being watched intensified. As he
crunched the hard biscuit, Tim scanned the surrounding woods
closely. The palms of his hands were sweaty, and he wiped
them on his denims, disgusted. It was not without reason he
had been nicknamed "Meeky." He had always been nervous in
tense situations. How he had had gumption enough to knock

Mike's jaw askew was a mystery. There had been no fear at all. His anger had been large enough to conquer fear. Seeing Ruth and Garrett together had snapped the chains that usually bound him.

But Garrett hadn't been the only one. What about Deputy Dwyer? When he butted up against the lawman and his .45, face to face, he had struck again. Maybe it was impulse, but he'd felt no fear then, either.

Tim sighed and wiped his hands again. No matter what had happened, he was slipping into the familiar role again: "Meeky."

Hardtack finished, Tim drank from the cool waters of Birch Creek, lit his pipe, and, still on foot, led Buck through the stubborn army of brush once more. He levered a shell into the rifle's chamber, setting the hammer at safety on half-cock. You never knew about bears. As big as they were, they could be as silent as the stars. Brush as thick as that through which he and Buck traveled was the worst kind. The thick growth gave no hint of bruin's presence, unless you smelled him. The brute lay in wait, like a block of granite, but pounced like a lynx when his victim moved into just the right position—usually from behind.

From the slowly changing topography of the countryside, Tim knew he must be close to Jake's cabin. A wooded promontory on the far side of Birch Creek was only a mile from the place, according to his friend. They were abreast of the promontory now, and Tim breathed more easily.

He rounded a difficult bend, where the trail was less than a couple of feet from the river. A steep bank rose along the inside of the trail but the willows had thinned somewhat, and his progress speeded up. And then, suddenly, the enemy was there. He was a large brown bear. The carnivore was standing on all fours, square in the center of the trail. He had a set, purposeful look about his slightly dished face. His small eyes glinted and the rough fur along his neck bristled. He was swaying in rhythm to a steady roll of growling and hisses, which increased in tempo as seconds passed.

Tim gasped and clutched the .45-70 to his chest. Buck, reins dangling, stiffened, eyes rolling. He snorted in fear and rose on his hind legs, whinnying and pawing the air. When he came down, he galloped over the back trail. The bear rolled into an immediate charge. Crackling through the brush, he was on Tim in seconds.

Tim fired from the waist. The four-hundred-grain slug bit deep into the bear's chest but failed to alter or slow the attack. Tim was knocked flat, and the browny swept on, after puncturing Tim's jeans with a couple of quick snaps. He wanted Buck, a figure of meat that he understood. Horse was the same as caribou or moose to him. But the sorrel had made his escape by then. He had stopped in the distance, dancing nervously, eyes on the bear, but safe. Even the bear knew that a chase would prove fruitless, so he turned his attention on the meat he had ignored at first: Tim.

In the confused moments after he was tumbled, Tim rolled over and came up on his knees. He pumped a cartridge into action and fired. The bear staggered this time and bawled, front paws flailing at the second wound. Then he plummeted toward Tim like the raging force of nature that he was.

Tim fired again. The rifle boomed, sending heaving echoes through the countryside, and Tim found himself inanely hoping that no human would hear.

If the bullet struck, there was no evidence, because a thousand pounds of lethal brown bear crashed into Tim, chewing and clawing. Entangled in the thick, coarse fur, Tim was nearly overpowered by the stench. It was a garbage-dump and cesspool odor combined, a stink he'd experienced from a distance before.

To fight back was useless, so Tim lay still, pretending he was dead. It was a trick he'd heard old-timers talk about, but he expected the end at any minute. He wondered what it would be like. As the surging body over him pressed closer, his senses flicked on and off like a faulty lamp. Did one know when he died? He was past fear at that point, and he developed the odd sensation of becoming an outside observer instead of the main attraction. Calmly, he waited for the great blackness, or whatever, but the hooded specter with the scythe waived the opportunity.

The three hot slugs of lead that had struck so forcefully were having a belated but fatal effect. Tim noticed a weakening in the blows, as the bear slid away. The growls changed to a strained longing for air. This went on for some seconds, then the browny lay still. His muzzle rested on a front paw, and his eyes were half shut. He seemed to be napping, save for a bloody foam bubbling at the corners of his jaws.

Tim rolled away and retrieved his rifle. He fired into the bear's massive head, and the great beast convulsed, half throwing his weight into the air. He fell back and a muscular shudder rippled through the body, ending with the animal spinning around and around on his side in a bloody circle. The spinning grew weaker, and finally the bear lay still, his glazed eyes fixed on the man who had introduced him to eternity.

Even at that terrible moment, when Tim himself wasn't sure just what kind of a game death intended to play, he felt pity. No creature of the wilderness had a chance against the weaponry of man. On the other hand, a man's life was only as good as his bullets when he met charging mayhem. He sat weakly on the body, noting with some surprise, how warm it was, soft and comfortable—and the next he knew he was sprawled on the ground, gazing at some clouds, which at that moment had chosen to look like the downtown business section of Fairbanks.

It took several head shakes for Tim to recall what had happened. The fight with the bear—was it a bad dream? Was he in bed? He moved sideways and came up against the reality of raw fur and knew this was no dream. He was deep into actuality, and he was hurt.

By careful manipulation, Tim managed to stand upright, using the bear's long fur as handholds. He moved his arms and legs experimentally, expecting to see bones protruding through flesh. But his arms and legs were intact. That could not be said for his ribs. His whole upper right chest burned, and where the clothing had been ripped away, he saw torn flesh. His clothing was shredded and bloody. Tim knew he was a hurt man, but he could thank God that he wasn't trotting alongside the bear on some heavenly highroad.

His head was giving trouble, senses fading in and out. During one of the "in" flashes, he noticed that Buck had returned. The horse was grazing uptrail a couple of hundred feet, and refused Tim's calls. He rolled his eyes, and snorted, but remained where he was.

Realizing that nothing in heaven or earth would entice Buck past the bear, Tim was forced to leave the horse. He turned for Jake's cabin while he still had strength and would have shouted for joy when he reached the place after a fifteen-minute staggered walk, but he had no voice to shout with. He lurched to the bunk and collapsed, and when he woke up the sun was sending pleasant messages through the cabin's only window.

Taking inventory, he found that his face was hamburger. The right cheek had been clawed, the left one bitten, and both wounds lay open and ugly. His upper right chest was also clawed and bloody, and from the feel of it, Tim figured several ribs had cracked. There was a long gash in the calf of his left leg, which might have been worse, except for high leather boots. From what he knew about bear attacks on humans, he'd gotten off easily. In fact, it was some kind of a miracle.

Snatching a bucket from the wash stand, Tim opened the door to get water and found Buck gazing peacefully at him. The horse had probably taken the high bank around the bear and dropped down when he was plenty clear. Buck carried a pack and there was a first-aid kit in it. Tim let the pack down and unsaddled the horse. He went for his water in the river and on returning rummaged in the pack until he found the kit. There were, also, three bottles of whiskey securely wrapped in blankets. Riley was a great believer in the medicinal value of spirits. And for that, Tim was grateful.

He started a fire, heated the water, and bathed his wounds in a solution of Sear's Family Soap. Then he doused them with whiskey, whooping at the sting. He was able to bind the leg wound, but could do nothing with either his face or his chest except clean them. What a mess! Of all the days for the bear to be on the prowl, it had to be when he, Timothy Meeker, was around!

A feeling that he'd have to return to Riley's for medical help increased his gloom. He was so weak, he'd probably fall off Buck and break his neck. And by now every lawman within two hundred miles was probably at Central, looking for him.

Yet, if he didn't get the face wounds stitched, he'd carry a couple of dandy scars for the rest of his life. And his ribs needed shoring up, taping of some kind. In addition to all of that, carnivores carried uncleanliness in their claws and teeth, and the danger of blood poison was real.

With his brain aching from these problems, Tim snatched the water bucket and headed for a refill. As he was sinking the bucket into the river, he saw a large, gray wolf watching him. The animal was so unexpected that Tim shivered with a thrill. He stared in fascination as the wolf gave play to a prodigious yawn, revealing rows of white teeth and a glistening red tongue. When their owner closed down again, the jaws snapped with a crack clearly audible above Birch Creek's busy swish. He returned Tim's stare for a moment, then casually trotted into the forest.

When Tim reached the cabin again, he lay down to rest. He lay quietly, thinking about the wolf, when another thought popped into mind: he had been afraid of the bear, but he hadn't panicked. Actually, he'd been pretty cool.

CHAPTER 5

When Tim awoke the next morning, his face was swollen and darkly purple. He could have been mistaken for a clown, but it was no clowning matter. In spite of the self-applied medical aid, he would have to go for help.

Fortunately, there was Riley. He had lived in the woods most of his life, just beyond the fingertips of civilization. It had fallen upon him to doctor the injured many times, and the old-timer's reputation as a "pretty good" practitioner was widespread.

Saddling Buck proved to be an outsized effort, and Tim was wringing wet when at length he climbed aboard. His mind was muggy, with just enough awareness left to know what must be done. As they began the journey, he yelped in pain when Buck's hoofs jarred. He complimented himself on having the wisdom to stick a quart of whiskey in the saddle bag. Had it not been for Old Crow, he would have fainted.

As they drew near the dead bear, Buck hedged. The great lump of a creature lay directly parallel to the narrow trail. Its fur rippled in a river breeze, and it seemed to Tim the bear was only sleeping, though he knew better.

He dismounted and painfully led the reluctant Buck around the mountain of flesh. The horse strained and rolled his eyes, but some of his fear of two days before had abated. But once broadside, the sorrel threw back his head and angled away. His hindquarters slipped into Birch Creek, and for a moment Tim thought he'd lost him. But the water wasn't deep, and Buck struggled out, still glaring and shivering.

In passing the bear, Tim noticed that its undersides had been ripped open. Something was feeding there, another meat eater. His muggy senses suddenly alert, Tim glanced around and saw the same wolf he'd seen the day before. The animal was on the high bank gazing down. He made no effort to run, but watched with slitted eyes.

"Hey," said Tim conversationally, "you can be a big help, if you eat all this old boy. He's going to stink up the country in a day or two and draw every critter for twenty miles. Get yours while you can."

In no mood for more talk, Tim led Buck up the trail and out of sight of the bear before mounting again. The horse calmed considerably, and seemed ready for cargo. After another pull on the bottle, Tim found himself wondering why it was horses were so panicky around bears. Most of them he knew would dive off a cliff to get away. Yet the wolf hadn't bothered Buck in the least. Or didn't seem to, anyway. Damned odd.

Though the willow growth slapped him with hellish accuracy, Tim made no attempt to guard his face. It took all his strength to keep his seat, and he let the willows have their way.

Once they left Birch Creek, the going was easier, and Buck made good time. By evening they were within a quarter of a mile of Riley's. Tim hitched Buck to a tree and approached the roadhouse on foot. He experienced the queer calm of *déjà vu*. I keep sneaking up on Riley's, he told himself. Will I play this game forever? Still, he had to make certain the way was clear.

The square log building seemed at peace. Smoke curled out of the chimney, and there was quiet in the yard. Even Riley's dogs were dozing atop their kennels. Tim's wounds were so agonizing that he threw further caution overboard and strode across the clearing. Not caring a damn, he crashed the door open. Two men were present. One was Riley. The other was Jake Lindstrum. Both looked up in surprise, which quickly changed to horror.

"Good God, man!" exclaimed Riley. "What happened?"

"Bear," grunted Tim, slumping into a chair.

Both men knew exactly what Tim's one word of explanation meant, and Jake had only a single question.

"Did you get him?"

Tim nodded.

"Good boy. Riley, we are going to need needle and thread."

The old-timer disappeared. Jake, in the meantime, helped the injured man shrug out of his clothes. He whistled softly as the chest and leg wounds came into sight.

"You were lucky," he said.

Tim nodded again but muttered, "Buck is tied on your trail. Take care of him, will you?"

Jake said he would, but Tim, wavering, repeated the request.

"Don't waste your breath," said Lindstrum. "Listen, you got more to worry about than Buck just now."

"Oh?"

"That's why I'm here. I was about to leave for the cabin."

"Oh?" said Tim again, not at all feeling conversational.

"Garrett is on the way out. He's got Tod Cowles, the deputy marshal, and Sike Hendrickson with him. And I hear Dwyer is on the way from Circle."

"Quite a crowd," said Tim from far away.

Riley returned with medical supplies and laid them on a table. First, he bathed the wounds in a warm boric acid solution. When they had been cleaned to his satisfaction, he placed a compress of fresh linen over the chest wounds, then bound the entire rib cage with wide adhesive tape. When he was through, Tim felt more of a piece.

Next, the old-timer bound the leg wound and after that he examined Tim's face.

"That's goin' to be a job, boy," he said gently and sloshed whiskey into a mug. "Drink that," he ordered, and Tim complied. Riley poured some more. "Hang on to that, you'll need it."

Riley produced a medium needle, and ran a length of white

cotton thread through its eye. He then sterilized the needle over a candle flame.

"All's I got is this here," he said, "but I had lots of practice sewing people back together and they turned out all right. No freaks, anyway."

Tim sipped the whiskey and sat rigid in his chair. He felt the bite of the needle and gripped the chair hard. He felt every inch of the thread drawing through his flesh, a dull pulling of internal surfaces, a long stretch of fiery pain. He wanted to scream, but he clenched his jaws shut. Sweat beaded his forehead, and he gripped the chair hard enough to draw juice out of it, his doctor later observed.

Riley worked quickly, aware that the longer a sewing job took, the more pain for the victim. He sewed with deft certainty, knowing from the experience of half a hundred similar occasions just how tight to draw the thread and just how many stitches to the inch.

At the end of the session, Tim was half drunk, and his eyes glazed from a combination of liquor and pain. But when Riley handed him a mirror, what he saw had been worth the trouble.

"Though I do look like a baseball," he complained.

"When you pull those threads out, you'll have a little scarrin', but not much," prophesied the old-timer, ignoring the complaint. "Just enough for reminders." And now that the doctoring was done, he took a hefty drink himself.

Outdoors, Riley's dogs set up a roar.

"Somebody's comin'," said the old man. "Tim, you get up in the loft. There ain't no time to hide you anyplace else."

He grabbed a rope hanging on a wall and pulled. A set of steps swung down, leading to a trapdoor. Tim climbed to the loft and shut the trapdoor after him. Riley let the steps up and hung the rope on its nail. Meanwhile, Jake cleaned away the medical supplies, and when the door opened, both men were reading comfortably by the barrel stove. Tim couldn't see, but he heard it all through the floorboards.

"Where's he at, Riley?" boomed Garrett.

"Where's who?" Riley shot back.

"You know damned well who. He got away from Dwyer, but he can't have gone far."

"If you mean Tim Meeker, he left for points south long ago."

"We saw nobody on the trail," intervened Cowles.

"Well, hell, he ain't exactly goin' to carry lights on him" was the salty reply.

"Easy," chimed in Hendrickson's silky voice. "We'll give the opinions here."

You haven't enough brain to give an opinion on a grasshopper, thought Tim bitterly.

"We plan to search around," said Garrett, and Tim envisioned the bowie-knife moustache curling up in a spasm of arrogance.

"You go right ahead," invited Riley, "but if you people so much as muss up a fryin' pan, I'll throw you out. Law or not!"

Tim grinned. You couldn't bluff that one.

"Don't get so hot," Tod Cowles advised. "We aren't going to 'muss' anything."

"What you doing here, Jake?" Garrett asked suddenly. "Just seeing you makes me suspicious. You and Meeky always been close."

"We were all close once," said Jake pointedly. "Don't challenge me, Mike. I'm not answerable to you."

Jake's tone was edged in steel, and Tim listened with more than a touch of envy. Why couldn't he talk to Mike like that!

"You and Meeky are still pretty thick," rumbled Garrett.

"So?" Lindstrum was defiant.

"So I figure you got him hid someplace. Don't you have a cabin around here?"

"Sure, Garrett. So?"

"Meeky's probably hiding under a bed in it."

"Want to go see?"

Jake was playing a bold hand, and Tim held his breath, but the fateful moment vanished with the arrival of Dwyer.

There was a brief exchange of greetings, then Dwyer said, "I didn't see a sign. Hell, by now he's had time to get to Valdez."

"We got people waiting there, too," said Cowles.

"Well, enough of talk," roared Garrett. "I want that man, so let's get cracking!"

I'll bet you want me, thought Tim.

"I'm offering three thousand dollars for him," said Garrett, "and that's payable to anybody, lawman or citizen. You could use the money, Jake."

"I'm rich," came the iron-clad reply. "What's he got on you, Garrett, that you offer that kind of money?"

There was a dead silence in the room. Tim could feel the tension through the floor. He knew that if they fought, Jake would win. He was as rawboned as a fence post, physically tougher than any man present. And he was absolutely fearless. Tim saw him kill an angry grizzly with a .22 rifle and show little emotion over it.

Sike Hendrickson must have made a move, because Tim heard Jake say, "Don't try it, Sike. I'd just as soon take you apart as look at you."

Dwyer cut in.

"Let's get on with why we're here," he said. "You people can fight later. Some of you go outside and hunt around. I'll look upstairs."

There was a dry rustle of clothing, as men suited words to action. Petrified, Tim looked frantically for a place to hide. The loft grudgingly borrowed light from below through some narrow cracks. In the gloom, Tim saw the dim outlines of some boxes. He ducked behind the largest and scrunched down as small as possible.

The steps swung down, and Dwyer opened the trapdoor. He entered the loft, pistol in hand.

"If you're here," he said to the darkness, "better come out.

You'll be safer with me than Garrett, by the looks of things."

Tim froze. Any sound from him meant passage to the jailhouse.

"I haven't forgotten what you did at Birch Creek," Dwyer went on. "I owe you one for saving my life. Give 'er up, and I'll see if I can't get the judge to go light."

"Do you think I'd be crazy enough to hide a man up there?" bellowed Riley from below. "That'd be the first place anybody would look."

"Yes," said Dwyer, "I think you'd be crazy enough."

He moved closer to Tim, scanning the shadows. Tim wished fervently that he was a mouse—it was no use trying to be as small as one. He was just too long and lank for that. His nose began to itch as the deputy moved ever closer. He could have reached out and touched the man's legs. His nose itched terribly, and a sneeze was building. Sure that discovery was imminent, the wanted man tensed. He planned to fight.

Dwyer stood quietly for perhaps a ten count, then Tim saw the legs retreat. The stairs creaked, and the trapdoor closed. The stairs swung back up, and he was alone again. He scratched his nose and thwarted the sneeze, but it had been too close for comfort.

"I didn't see nobody," he heard Dwyer mutter. "Thought sure he'd be there."

"I told you!" barked Riley.

"Yeah, well . . . Did you know he saved my life?"

"We heard you talking," said Jake.

"I already knew about it, when . . ." Riley cut himself off.

"When Meeker stopped after leaving me stranded?" There was more than a touch of irony in Dwyer's question.

"You knew he'd stop!" declared the old-timer.

"But you didn't bother to notify us."

"Now how in the world am I going to 'notify' anybody from here? No wireless in Central, Dwyer."

"How convenient" was the weighted reply.

There was a scuffing of feet, then the deputy said, "Think I'll join the others. It'll go hard on you, Riley, if we find him."

A door opened and shut, and in the silence that followed, Tim thought about what had happened. Had Dwyer seen him but let him go, to pay back a debt? Or had he actually escaped in the gloom? They'd been less than two feet apart. How could the man have missed him?

Jake and Riley were whispering down below, probably planning. Fifteen minutes passed, then Garrett entered with Sike and the deputies.

"He's around," charged Garrett bluntly. "I know Meeky, and how his mind works. He runs scared most of the time. Hell," the big man scoffed. "He wouldn't have the guts to cut back to Fairbanks. He's around, and I mean to get him. Did you check upstairs?"

"Yes," said Dwyer, "I checked."

"Good?"

"You can take my word for it, Garrett" was the even reply. "Nobody's there."

"Just asking," grunted Garrett. "Don't get insulted."

The next voice belonged to Tod Cowles.

"Garrett, what's all the deal? Meeker's so-called crimes aren't that bad you need to offer three thousand to anybody."

"Don't you worry about it!" snapped Garrett. "The reward is my own business. You were assigned to help, not ask stupid questions."

"So be it," said Cowles. "Where next? The Springs?"

Tim knew the deputy was referring to Circle Hot Springs, eight miles away on a spur road.

"Yeah" from Garrett. "I doubt he's there, but we better have a look."

There was movement, and the door slammed. A few moments later, horses thumped out of Central, but Riley didn't lower the stairs for a long time. When he did, he posted Jake at a side window overlooking the Hot Springs trail.

Tim descended quickly, tense with the strain, his face aching badly.

"What next?" he asked.

"You get back down on Birch Creek, pronto."

"I'll come see you when this blows over," Jake called from the window. "That Dwyer must have been blind."

"Thank God," said Riley.

"Amen," agreed Tim.

Riley made a pack for Tim. More food, another couple of bottles, and more shells for the .45-70.

The pack had just been finished, when the door opened and an Indian girl entered. She looked the men over carefully. Her eyes remained on Tim's face, but she spoke to Riley. "I come from Circle an' head for Hot Springs. You got food?"

The old-timer nodded, as Tim and the girl stared at each other. She was tall, Tim noted, with very dark eyes and hair. Her cheekbones were prominent under taut skin, her mouth was wide and generous, and her nostrils flared slightly above a square chin. The picture was one of solidity rather than beauty, except for the dark eyes, which danced with a light of their own.

Right now, the eyes were fascinated by Tim's face, and the girl spoke. "What you do? Fight bear maybe?"

Tim nodded.

"Yeah, I thought that. You kill him?"

"Yes."

The girl's eyes glowed. "He got you, eh?"

"He banged me around, yes."

"Hey! It take a big man to fight bear."

At that point, Riley grasped the girl by the arm and led her off. The old man motioned to Tim to get out. After a quick eyeball reconnaissance, Tim darted over to Jake's trail and made his way to Buck.

Once astride the sorrel, he pondered events. Garrett was running scared no doubt. That was something, anyway. Apparently, the whole interior of Alaska knew of the incident by now, and with three thousand dollars on his head, he'd become fair game for every trapper, prospector, and villager in the region. That was not so good. He'd have to lay not only low, but way low until he could think of something to get him out of what was getting to be a more and more scary situation as the days passed.

Tim thought of his strange encounter with the Indian girl. She seemed to have a large interest in bears. What was she doing by herself in Central? Indians usually traveled in pairs, rarely by themselves. Interesting.

Uppermost in Tim's mind, though, was Garrett. His ex-partner wanted him very much, and there was no doubt in Tim's thinking about how the man with the bowie-knife moustache wanted him: either alive or dead would be just fine. And probably, dead was his personal preference.

CHAPTER 6

Tim found his way to Jake's cabin without trail trouble, but he was exhausted. Though reasonably sure that Garrett and the rest didn't know about the place, he half expected to see the big man pop out from every bush and that didn't make for easy riding. And it was weird, knowing that somebody wanted you dead—particularly when that somebody had been a friend of long standing.

Aside from nightmarish thoughts, there were no problems, and the cabin rose out of the forest like home sweet home. After tending to Buck, Tim hit the blankets and slept until noon the next day. He had a leisurely breakfast of ham and eggs and coffee. Riley had wrapped a dozen eggs in a blanket along with the other supplies. The eggs were as strong as the onions they shared warm storage with, but Tim ate heartily. Tainted eggs were the least of his worries.

After breakfast, he worked at cleaning the cabin. Jake, like most trappers, found little time for tidying up.

The cabin was small—maybe, Tim guessed, ten by fourteen inside. Small areas required less wood for heating, thus saving time at the woodpile. The floor was dirt, well packed, almost shiny with use. There were a couple of smooth boards by the bunk to rest the feet on, a luxury most trappers didn't allow. One didn't cart a scarce commodity like lumber through the wilds for such foolishness. Good boards, meaning any boards, were building material. But the two Jake placed beside his bed were a nicety he didn't feel wasteful.

"Hell," he told Tim once, "that dirt floor is cold!"

All the furniture was homemade, and there was little of it: one small table, one chair, and one bunk, which doubled as a daytime lounge. Pots and pans hung from nails driven into the log walls near the stove. And a washstand with basin occupied a space near the door. A cupboard, constructed of the luxury item, lumber, graced a wall. It held a few dishes, but little food. Most of Jake's food was stored in a nearby cache.

The cabin and grounds were functional, no more, no less. There was, also, a slight, fetid odor of dead animals. Jake skinned his catch in the cabin and stretched the fur there as well. He laid it to dry on pole racks hung from the ceiling. It was his plan to build a regular skinning shed, but that remained a plan and Tim doubted it would ever bear fruit. You got used to the stink of dead animals in time, so what the hell?

For the first couple of days, though, Tim left the door wide open to air the place. The smell left him queasy. The airing helped some, but at the end of the second day, mosquitoes discovered Tim. After spending a miserable night, he slammed the door, and it remained shut from then on. Better the stench of death than the pitiless whine of a hundred mosquitoes each clamoring for its drop of blood.

Tim's wounds healed well, but he couldn't shave. The rising stubble slowly turned into a beard. It was the first he'd ever had, and he was surprised when it matured into a curly red mass. His hair was light—dishwater blond, he called it—and the contrast was startling. He was not a little pleased, though he chided himself about vanity. There was a real benefit from the beard, that of disguise. With long hair not even Garrett would recognize him, and he decided to make the whiskers temporarily permanent.

On more than one occasion he saw the gray wolf. The animal never ventured into the clearing, but paused at the edge of the forest. Because his tail was dark, Tim picked the name of Blacktail for him. When the wolf's mate appeared, he called her Yellowchest, because of her markings. She didn't show up often, and Tim judged she had pups to watch.

Once, he whistled at Blacktail to see what would happen. The animal's ears perked, and he glanced sharply at Tim. He raised his sharp muzzle, sniffing, then trotted into the forest.

Tim was not afraid of wolves. Though he'd heard terrible stories about their enmity toward man, he doubted much of what was supposed to be true. Any he'd ever seen, and there were many in the Panhandle, seemed less than aggressive, more curious than feisty. Unlike bears, who for Tim spelled arrogance in capital letters, wolves were withdrawn. He was woods-wise enough to realize wolves could be dangerous, as any free animal can be dangerous, but he nevertheless admired their ability to survive. In the face of rifle, traps, and bounties, as well as natural enemies, the wolf persevered. It never occurred to him to aim his gun at Blacktail, though he might have shot a bear on sight. Tim acknowledged that wasn't exactly fair to the bruin tribe, but that was the way the matter had come to set with him. After all, he now had scars to prove his thesis that bears were a brutish bunch.

The browny he had killed was having his own revenge, as he'd expected. The decaying carcass stank, and since there was a lot of carcass, the stench lingered and thickened. It seemed to Tim he could taste it in his soup. The bear's revenge was powerful.

Finally he saddled Buck and led him to the body. Though the horse shied away from close contact, Tim tied a long rope to the bear's forearm and to the pommel. Between the two of them, Buck pulling and him prying, they managed to tumble the maggot-eaten corpse into the fast-moving waters of Birch Creek.

Though Tim was satisfied by this, he soon discovered that the bear was not through with him. The body caught on a sand-bar just below the cabin and hung there for two days, turning the atmosphere blue. He was forced to get his drinking water above the great, water-soaked lump, until heavy rain in the hills raised the river. The bear then broke loose and tumbled heavily downstream, legs windmilling ponderously until they disappeared.

"Next time I shoot a bear," he informed Buck, "I'll arrange to do it in Garrett's back yard. No—I'll do it in Ruth's front yard." Tim grinned at the picture. "I'll shoot three of them, by God! And leave an extra."

To pass the evenings, he read from a set of Shakespeare's *Complete Works*. They were on a shelf over the bunk and were companioned with Cooper's *Leatherstocking Tales, Modern Blacksmithing,* and *The Home Mechanic.*

As did most trappers, Jake supplied himself with plenty of reading, a hedge against loneliness. He had little time for reading, especially when the fur was running good, but that little did sneak in once in a while. He never traveled the line in anything under fifty below or in bad storms.

"I like to improve what mind I got," he once said.

Jake's was not a bookish brain, and Tim suspected his friend spent more time with the technical books than the classics. For that matter, Tim didn't understand half of what Shakespeare said himself, and he thought Cooper was drier than a popcorn hiccup. He ended by browsing in the blacksmithing text and read more about the art than he really wanted to know, but it was a way to fill the hours.

In mid-June Jake Lindstrum paid a visit. Tim, sagging a bit in the morale section from the isolation, was glad to see the man's long and lean frame push through the door early one evening.

He presented Tim with a copy of the *Fairbanks Times*. It devoted much of the front page to "Mike Garrett, local businessman and philanthropist, lately betrayed by his trusted partner and boyhood friend, Timothy Meeker." Garrett's visage grinned at the world as he was handing a slip of paper to a woman in a nun's habit.

Tim threw the newspaper down without reading more, shouting, "Now who is that lovely philiothroanthropist kissing up to?"

"Mr. Big is handing a check to Sister Theresa. The money is to build a new wing on St. Joseph's Hospital. Naturally, they plan to call it the 'Garrett Addition.' "

Tim growled when he heard that and yelled again, "Is that what people think of me—a betrayer?"

"Aw, that's just newspaper talk," said Jake soothingly. "They got to sell papers."

"But they're making money off my bad luck. They've known me for years; don't they know I'd never 'betray' anybody, for Pete's sakes?"

Jake shrugged. "Don't let it get you."

But Tim ranted on.

"And where does that big-spender get the money? He ought to be broke. Remember, I burned him out."

"Well, maybe you ought to get busy and show Garrett up for what he really is."

"I've got to!"

"But not yet, I'd say."

"Meaning?"

"Listen, Garrett's got everybody on his side just now. He and your darling Ruth. You better have some pretty good evidence. Hell, you couldn't hang a murder rap on Garrett now if he did it in plain sight of the governor." Jake paused. "And speaking of politics, Mike is setting up a campaign to get elected mayor in November."

"And Ruth? Is she faithfully by his side?" Tim asked, feeling the sting of jealousy.

"I hate to tell you this, but, yes, she is. The two of them make a fine couple."

"The belle of the ball, is that it?"

"Not just that, old buddy. She's the mistress of Fairbanks. She gives the fanciest soirees in town, and you know what that means. She's at the top of the social pile."

"And I put her there!" shouted Tim. "Not Garrett, but me. I introduced her to those people, damn it, Jake. And all the time she was holding me by one hand, she was picking my pocket with the other."

Jake opened a bottle he brought, and they each had a drink.

"What you figure on doing?" Jake asked, after they'd both warmed up a bit.

Tim frowned.

"I don't know just exactly. I got to prove my innocence by showing Mike's guilt. He's got records of his dirty dealing someplace, I'd bet my poke on that. If I can find those, Garrett's goose will be baked."

Jake poured more whiskey.

"How do you plan to find the records?"

"I don't know—maybe get in the office files, though I don't think he keeps them there. It's a place to start, though."

Tim knew he was talking about a long shot, but it was all he had. The outlook was gloomy.

The bottle dropped another inch, and talk gradually drifted to old times in Juneau. Better days, it seemed to Tim, when the sun was always shining. They were young, boys, and they dreamed the great dreams. Life was spelled with a capital "L" then.

Juneau was an exciting place, a city of large participation in Alaska's history. It was from Juneau that the move toward the great wealth of the interior began. Joe Juneau and Dick Harris, a couple of prospectors, founded the camp in 1880. Prospectors grubstaked there before heading north to Prince William Sound, to the Yukon River, the Forty Mile, and to a great arc of distant camps in the interior. Juneau remained an important supply base until the Klondike rush of 1897 and '98, when a new town, a seaport called Skagway, was born at the head of Lynn Canal. And though Juneau remained an important regional center, its influence as a supply depot decreased.

"I remember that Klondike rush like it was yesterday," said

Tim. "My dad left the first time he heard about gold. He had •
the fever bad."

"Yeah, my daddy, too," recalled Jake, "and, for that matter,
Garrett's old man went along with the rest."

"He also went broke," remembered Tim, "belly up."

Everything they spoke about in relation to Juneau carried an
involvement with Mike. He had been one of them; the three
had been friends for all of their young lives. Share and share
alike. If one had money, the others none, suddenly, they all had
money, no holding back.

"What happened?" Tim wondered aloud. "What happened
to the guy?"

"You were making more than wages at the Aurora," said
Jake.

"So?"

"Maybe the dough went to his head?"

Tim pondered. He had to agree to some extent. It had even
influenced him, so why not Garrett. But there hadn't been that
much, actually, though the income was damned high.

"Maybe it's power," said Jake.

Again Tim agreed, but had to ask, "If it's power he wants,
meaning political position, why would he jeopardize himself
playing the crook?"

There were no answers to that one, and Garrett remained an
enigma as the talk drifted to other matters. Jake brought up the
subject of a large, gray wolf.

"He's been hanging around here for a couple of years," said
the trapper, "and I got to get him. He's smart and won't touch
any of my sets, but that rascal's been ruining a lot of fur. He
eats the catch, and he lifts a leg on what he doesn't eat."

"Insult to injury," observed Tim.

"Right!"

"I saw him," Tim admitted and then for some reason was
sorry he said it.

"Listen." Jake knotted a fist. "If you nail that son of a bitch, I'll be forever grateful."

"I owe you that, my friend."

The next morning, Jake left early, and after his departure, the space he so vitally occupied in the cabin became a vacuum for Tim. The devils of isolation attacked, and a high-level depression wrestled his mind to a standstill before the sun had sucked the morning mists from Birch Creek.

He lounged around the cabin half the day, mulling over events. He'd come a long way to nowhere in just a few years. What in the world was he doing in a cabin miles from no place at all! What would have happened had he stood up to Mike when he first discovered his partner's crooked deals? Would he be here now? Suppose he'd gotten whipped, really beaten, would that have been as bad as he'd been given? Better to meet trouble head on than to run. If you ran, you didn't escape. The trouble just got worse. What *was* there about Garrett that had him bluffed?

To get away from his gloom, Tim walked along the river. As he listened to its cheerful murmur, the knot in his gut loosened, but returned when he remembered the news story about Garrett. His cheeks turned hot with embarrassment. He had acted like a child when he read it. What a way for a man to fight by hollering in the wind!

Tim picked up a rock and slung it across the river. Think! Think! Think! A man's mind could drive him crazy with *think!* And *think* didn't solve anything. Only action would do that.

Still gloomy, Tim retraced his steps toward the cabin, when he saw Blacktail. The wolf was poised at the edge of the forest as usual, one foot raised tentatively, his tail at half cock.

Remembering his promise to Jake, Tim loped to the cabin and hauled out the .45-70. He levered a shell into the chamber and aimed. The wolf's broad head came into the open sights, and Tim gently squeezed the trigger.

Blacktail never lowered his amber eyes, but stared at Tim

with unblinking steadiness. As his finger tightened, Tim couldn't help but notice the animal's lack of fear. It was apparent that he had no idea death separated him from the living by a simple, single gesture.

For a frozen moment, man and wolf faced each other, and in the end the man lowered his weapon. He didn't want to shoot Blacktail, and he knew it. The animal had come to mean something in his life. At least he was company, by God! Maybe not very close company, not even what could be called friendly, but he was *there*.

As Tim hung the rifle back on its peg, his conscience tried to interfere. He was letting a friend down. The wolf had caused Jake pain and cost him money. The friend had done much, and he owed Jake a lot more than the life of one wolf.

But conscience fought a losing battle. The most Tim would concede was noninterference. If Jake shot the animal, all right, but he wouldn't do it himself.

To fill the days that followed, Tim cut wood for Lindstrum's woodpile. After ten cords he quit. Jake wouldn't use that much in two years. He built an outhouse, because there wasn't one. Jake tied a log between two trees over a pit, a "Swede" toilet. Hell for mosquitoes in summer and just as much hell for frostbite in fifty below.

After the outhouse, he ran out of jobs, so he hiked. He was often gone all day, lunching on hardtack and canned meat. He found that the country below the cabin was a good part meadowland, with rich dirt. It would take a plow easily. And all along Birch Creek's banks, tall spruce reached for the clouds. Fine cabin logs.

A number of small creeks fed into Birch, and the reluctant outlaw panned them. He found a few colors, but nothing more. Even as he washed the gravel in a frying pan borrowed for the purpose, he knew chances of finding gold were as remote as finding pinfeathers in a football. The Birch Creek country had its own gold rush in the 1890s. It was short-lived, but for a while the ground for fifty miles around had been scoured by hundreds of professional prospectors. When the golden Klondike bared its treasures, few miners remained on the Birch, where only a few streams paid.

One thing the creeks did yield was tender-fleshed grayling, a silvery, big-finned trout. Tim found dry flies and line in Jake's cabin, and he made a rod from a willow. He caught all the fish he wanted on a day-to-day basis. Deep fried in bacon grease, they were as tasty a food as he ever hoped to find.

But in spite of gourmet trout, long hikes, which he loved, and all outdoors to wander in, he admitted after a month that Garrett wasn't his worst enemy just then: boredom was. By nature he was an open-spirited man, one who enjoyed company. The isolation of the wilds, even with all its beauty, brought increasing loneliness. Beauty, to be truly appreciated, must be shared, and he longed for the sound of voices, a rubbing of shoulders.

Finally, he convinced himself that he had to see Riley. His wounds needed attention, and he should find out what was going on in Fairbanks. Had Garrett married Ruth? Was the law still looking for him?

His beard by now was fairly well grown. It was a curly, red bramble bush that hid his face well, save for the scars. Convinced that his trip was not only necessary, but put off much too long, he left for Central at six in the morning. How nice it would be to hear the music of a human voice. Even the old-timer edginess of Riley's.

CHAPTER 7

When Tim entered Riley's roadhouse, he was greeted by the proprietor with damp enthusiasm.

"You crazy?" demanded the old-timer. "Any minute now this place could draw more lawmen than a hoedown in a cathouse!"

Tim was dismayed. Riley had seen through his disguise at once. If he could, so could Garrett. The disguise needed work.

"Riley, you know I'm not that important an outlaw."

"Maybe not, but that three-thousand-dollar bounty has been upped to four thousand, son, and that makes you glitter." With a turn of mischief, he added, "Could use it myself."

"So Garrett upped the price," said Tim thoughtfully. "He wants me bad."

"Three thousand was bad" came the observation. "Four thousand is worse than bad. Every man within five hundred miles of Fairbanks is your jailer. And I don't think Garrett would cry if you were brought in dead."

Tim, a bit nettled by Riley's acid tone, turned on a little heat.

"And what about you?" he asked. "Like you said, you could probably use four thousand, right?"

The old-timer laughed caustically, but his voice softened. "That was mean of me, boy, but I want you safe, not flittin' around like a duck with a singed ass."

"First time I been away from the cabin in a month," objected Tim. "I'd hardly call that flitting."

He stayed at the roadhouse for the rest of the day. By evening he was playing thrum-thrum on the kitchen table with his fingers. He'd drunk so much coffee that new depth had been added to the outhouse trail by his boots. He finally came to the obvious conclusion that he wasn't exactly an honored guest. Riley seemed, and probably rightly, apprehensive. Tim didn't fault that. He was, after all, a wanted criminal, and his friend was, in effect, harboring him. The law frowned on that, and you could push even a solid friendship just so far.

"Think I'll go over to the Springs place," Tim announced, after a supper of smoked whitefish and boiled potatoes.

Riley exploded.

"Damn it all, Tim! You mean you're pantin' for a *resort?* Man, you ought to lay low, and you know it."

Remembering how quickly Riley had recognized him under his thick beard, Tim decided on improving his disguise. He borrowed a pair of dark glasses from Riley, and a thick mackinaw. To top it off, he also filled a packsack and hoisted it to his back.

"How do I look?" he asked the old man.

"Like a danged cheechako," muttered Riley, "but it'll probably do."

"It isn't likely that anybody will be there who knows me, anyway," said Tim.

"How about your voice?" asked Riley. "Hell, boy, there's always somethin' that gives a man away."

"I'll keep my eyes open and my mouth shut. Shoot, I just want a change. Booze won't get me. I'll behave."

Riley nodded, but said, "When are you goin' to do something?"

"You mean about Garrett?"

"That's what I mean, boy. You just can't slide along like an otter on a mudbank. This here is a serious matter."

"Yeah. Well, I got a plan."

"Look, I know it gets lonely in the woods. We all get the lonesomes sometimes, but if you're looking for a cure, forget the Springs. That's like a weasel getting friendly with a number ought trap."

Tim knew his friend was right, but now that the Springs idea was in his head, he had to go see.

"Tell you what," he said. "Like I say, I have a plan. It's been waiting for my disguise to grow. I'll go into Fairbanks in a couple of weeks, all right?"

Riley accepted that and offered more coffee, but Tim declined, heading for the door. "Take care of Buck for me," he said. "I'll walk to the Springs, since Buck might be recognized."

The old-timer agreed. He could put the horse in a dark stall and blanket him. If the law came, maybe it wouldn't look too hard.

"Just don't be too long," he said. "I sometimes feel like I'm setting on a box of dynamite."

It was eight miles to Circle Hot Springs, and Tim didn't hurry. He puzzled over Riley's attitude, his provoked urging. It was true, he'd have to do something soon. It hadn't occurred to him before that his friend might be under any tension in regards to himself. He wasn't being fair to Riley or, for that matter, to Jake. Jake was under the gun, too, because of the cabin. Lindstrum could claim he had no idea, but he'd come under suspicion. Time was running out.

It was late when he arrived at the Springs. Frank Leach the owner had lately built a three-storied frame hotel, the most imposing structure in a hundred and fifty miles.

Leach, a square-built man with craggy eyebrows and a firm handshake, was at the desk.

"You walk from Central, stranger?" he asked.

"My horse went lame," explained Tim.

"Couldn't Riley lend you a nag?"

Tim shook his head, playing it carefully. "Riley needs his horses, and all that's left are his dogs." He glanced outside at the late sun and leafy trees. "And this is the time of poor sledding."

Leach grinned. "Well, a walk don't hurt nobody. That's the trouble with young 'uns today. They think they got to ride everwheres." He slapped his thighs. "These old pins have carried me far. They chased over these hills for years, till I got this place." The grin widened. "I found more gold in this hotel than I ever found in the ground."

"It's nice," offered Tim, looking around.

"Yep. Lots of work running it, but, hell, what's a man to do if he don't work?"

Tim agreed with that and climbed the stairs to his room. So far, so good. There weren't many at the Springs just then. Most people were at their mines, taking advantage of the short summer. They'd play when freeze-up closed their operations. Alaska was strictly seasonal country.

He found a towel and went to the pool, leaving the glasses and mackinaw. With so few present, Tim felt safe. The pool was housed in a log building at the rear of the hotel. The water smelled of sulfur and was hot enough to soften saddle leather, but Tim luxuriated. It was the first real bath he'd enjoyed since he'd been hiding. Even if the water did smell like bad eggs, Tim thought it was fine.

He soaked for half an hour, until a weakness came over him from the relaxing effect of liquid heat. Then he dried, dressed, and returned to the main building. The barroom was empty, which was good, and he ordered a beer.

Frank Leach served him.

"I do it all," he said with his happy grin. "Bartender to mortgage signer, that's me." He headed toward the door. "I got to tend some plumbing," he added. "This whole place is heated with springs water—cheap, but I haven't got all the kinks straightened out."

Tim voiced approval.

"If I don't get back, and you want more beer, help yourself. You can pay later."

The hotelkeeper left, and Tim was alone. He wondered if

he'd ever trust a customer of the Aurora's like Leach did him. After considering the thought, he nodded. Yes, there were some he could trust that way. Alaskans seemed to be an honest bunch. Except if your name was Garrett. Or Meeker.

He sipped his Olympia and let his thoughts roam, when music interrupted. He turned to see an Indian girl examining phonograph records in a shadowy corner. She was the same one he'd seen a month earlier at Riley's.

"Why don't you bring the records over here?" he called. "Better light near the bar."

She glanced up. "I see all right."

"Suit yourself."

Tim returned to his beer, remarking to himself that women were certainly uppity in this neck of the woods.

"Are you the man kill the bear?" the girl asked suddenly.

Tim swung around to be met by a pair of curious dark eyes.

How had she recognized him? His back had been turned toward her most of the time. And even though he'd left his glasses in the room, his beard should have been enough disguise to hide his identity from a relative stranger.

She must have sensed his hesitation, because she added, "Hey! I know your voice. I don't forget man who kills bears in fight."

Tim nodded.

"And he get your face good, huh? You grow beard to cover scars maybe?"

Again Tim nodded.

"What else that bear do?"

"He cracked four or five ribs."

She placed the records on a stand near the phonograph and walked to the bar.

"I like to see those ribs."

Tim stared.

"You mean take off my shirt?"

"Yes. Please."

In the atmosphere of the bar, a low-key shadowed square of burlap-walled intimacy, Tim found it easy to relax. The beer helped loosen inhibitions he might have ordinarily mustered. The idea of stripping to the waist to please an Indian girl's curiosity appealed to him, so he peeled off his shirt. His torso was still wrapped in Riley's tape, but hot water had loosened it.

"I think this adhesive-plaster case I'm in needs to come off," he said.

"I get scissors," offered the girl, "and take it off."

"Oh, I didn't mean that," objected Tim, embarrassed.

"I do it."

The girl met Tim's eyes directly. "My name is Molly Jack. I work here for Leach, make beds and like that, to get money."

She disappeared, leaving Tim to sip his beer and to think about her. He liked what he'd seen so far. She returned quickly with a large pair of shears and cut the tape deftly.

"Why do you want money?" Tim asked conversationally.

"I go Outside and get education."

"What do you want to study?"

"Oh, secretary, I thinks. That is good job."

She worked swiftly, without more talk. When the tape had been cut its breadth, she pulled at it gently. Tim winced as the adhesive stung his tender skin, but he'd been wondering about the wounds. Had Riley been more receptive, he'd have taken the case off there. The old man had cleaned the wounds well, but that was over a month ago and it had been a long time since they'd known fresh air.

The skin was wrinkled and pink around the injuries, but otherwise everything was in good shape. There would be scars, but there was no evidence of infection.

"I feel funny." Tim stretched, expanding his rib cage. "After being bound up so tight, I feel like I'm going to fly apart."

Molly reached over and touched his skin.

"So white," she said, "and so skinny." She giggled.

Red-faced, Tim shrugged back into his shirt. "I'm not skinny," he protested, "just not fat is all."

"Hey, another beer help that maybe."

"Good idea. Will you have one?"

Molly glanced at the door through which Leach had recently disappeared.

"My boss, I don't think he like that."

"Why not? You aren't on the job at this hour, are you?"

The Indian girl shook her head.

"Just the same, I think no. That other white man, he try to buy me beer, but Frank tell him no."

"Well, I don't want to get you in trouble, Molly . . ." Tim stopped. "What other man?"

"Oh, that one with the ice eyes, you maybe know him. He around here when I see you at Riley's."

"Was his name Sike Hendrickson?"

Molly nodded. "That is him." She shivered. "He look at me like I am animals, I think."

"I'm glad Frank was here."

"My boss, he is good."

Tim nodded. "Then how can I repay you for doing a dirty job for me?"

The black hair tossed.

"I don't need, what you say 'repay.' Listen, my people they don't like bears, see? Anybody who fight one he is like hero, you know? Bears, they bother us at fish camps lots of times. They eat our fish. They kill us, too, when they mad."

"They're bad, all right," Tim agreed. "That one who came at me, it was him or me, all right." He held his nose. "First time I ever smelled a bear so close. Ach!"

Again Molly Jack giggled. "Like what you call 'outhouse'?"

"Worse than that. You can put an outhouse, rotten guts, and garbage all together and they would be sweet perfume compared to that bear."

Molly nodded, delight in her broad features.

"Ah! My father, he fight bear once and say the same thing. Ahhhhh-deeee! Smell terrible." Molly pinched her nostrils between thumb and forefinger and added, "Whuuuuuuu-eeeeee!

"Listen," she went on, "I don't mean to be not nice awhile ago."

"That's all right."

"Indian woman, they have to be careful. White men, they want to marry us, but without preacher."

Tim didn't know much about Indian girls. There were many in the Panhandle, but he'd never mixed with them. The two societies, white and native, didn't mingle. If he knew little about white girls, he knew even less about Indians. They could have come from another planet.

"Well," he said lamely, "I wasn't thinking about marrying you without a preacher."

That wasn't entirely true, but he didn't elaborate.

"Maybe not," said the girl, and Tim knew she was assessing him. "I take that beer."

"What?"

"I have that beer now."

"What about Leach?"

"Oh, we go to your room, more private there."

Tim nodded. Maybe things would work out better than he'd hoped for. He stuffed his pockets with long-necked Olympia bottles and, taking Molly by the arm, led the way. The lobby was vacant, Leach was nowhere in sight, and they reached his room without being seen. Tim felt an excitement rising.

"I stay only for little while," said Molly. "Just to talk, you know?"

Tim opened a beer for each of them, then sat on the bed. Molly sat on the only chair, or rather, Tim noticed, she perched.

They sipped and said nothing, Tim planning how to proceed. A grandfather clock bonged once in the lobby, and Tim wondered who took the trouble to cart such a monster all the way from civilization.

Time passed. Finally, Tim whispered, for he suspected the walls were very thin, "You are going to become a secretary?"

"That's what I want."

"Have you had any training?"

"You mean can dumb Indian read and write?" The black eyes were triumphant. "You bet! I go to St. James Episcopal Mission in Tanana. I go there five years." Molly held up the fingers of one hand. "That is a lot more than most, but I learn lots. The Godmen there they like me and teach special."

Then she added with heat, "I will make myself somethings, you know what I say?"

"I think I do."

"Naw! You don't know. You only thinks you do. White people they different. Listen, I was born in a Yukon River fish camp. There were ten kids my mother had, and I was sixth. There are only four kids left."

"What happened?" Tim found he was really interested. That Molly spoke the truth, he had no doubt. Her very earnestness left no room for exaggeration.

"The others born sick, some of them, and they die. One year we have no meat and no fish, and two die then. I going to fix that!"

Tim, on his third or fourth beer, was feeling good, if fuzzy. The beer was strong. He found himself growing more and more attracted to the tall, rawboned Indian girl, who spoke so confidently about her future plans. What a difference between Molly Jack and Ruth Claxton! Ruth, with her sophistication and sly mind . . .

"I hope you do good," he said, opening another beer for her. She shook her head, but when he insisted, she shrugged, and said just one more. Beer did funny things to her, she explained. Bad things.

"Liquor is no good for native folk. It has evil. People in my tribe, sometimes they gets booze from Fort Yukon or Tanana maybe. Sometimes they make their own." Molly shuddered. "It is what you call 'bootlegger,' eh? You know it?"

Tim nodded. He did, indeed, know about bootleg whiskey—or Garrett did.

"No good from booze," Molly went on excitedly. "My people drink, they don't want to hunt or fish. They make no cache for winter, and they starve." Her face was somber. "I see that myself. Lots of them drink to death. They can't stop."

Tim, listening, marveled at the undertones in Molly's voice. It was a melody of womanly rhythm, earnest and determined, a young song of hope. She was going to make it all well for her people. She was a reformer, with a heart full of warm zeal, and her eyes glowed with the conviction that she and her people would lead the good life. All she needed was an education. Somehow that would open doors on a new springtime for her tribe, a starting over, and a never-looking-back at the bad times.

She appraised him. "What you do for a living?"

Without thinking, Tim said, "I own a tavern in Fairbanks."

Molly threw up her hands. "Ahh-deee! You are one of them?"

"Yes," Tim admitted, but hastened to add, "I don't like to see Indians have booze, either. I come from Juneau. It is bad for natives there, too."

Molly stared.

"Hey," she said, lowering her voice, "are you that guy who they are looking for? I hear them ask Frank Leach."

Tim realized his mistake too late. He could have bitten off his tongue. He'd let down his guard, thinking about what he wanted from Molly. She sat upright in the chair, her back arched in a graceful curve. He was very much aware of the femininity so close to him.

"Are you going to turn me in to the law?"

"Hah!" She gave a fierce mock-spit and glared. "Indians have nothing to do with white man's law. They make laws to suit them, not us. We go to some places where we fish for a hundred years, and they tell us no. We fish there anyway, and they arrest us. We hunt some moose, and they tell us not now, it ain't right season. Season? What is that? Season is when belly is empty, and we get moose then. White man's law arrest for that, too."

The girl tilted her bottle and drank. Tim noted the smoothness of her throat, which had a startling pallor in contrast to the tanned darkness of her face.

When the bottle came down with a thud, it was empty, and she signaled Tim to open another. Tim obeyed hastily. He was beginning to sense success.

"You white men are hard for Indian to understand," Molly went on, with a wave of the bottle. "The Godmen at the mission, they are good. They teach us and give us medicine. When we are hungry, they feed us, too. Oh, lots of times. Then your lawmen, they tell us not to do anything, not to live like we always live. If we do, they throw us in jail or take money away. That is bad, and they are bad men. Why is that, huh?"

She was growing angrier by the minute, as her inhibitions lessened. Tim, fearful that an outburst would arouse guests or, worse, attract Leach, spoke softly in an effort to calm her.

"It is hard to understand. There are so many rules that even white people don't understand all of them."

He placed a hand over hers. "Why don't you sit next to me on the bed?"

Molly jerked her hand away, and Tim discreetly withdrew his. Too early. Maybe after another beer or two.

"Don't do that" came the warning. "I like you, see, but not that much."

Molly's smoky eyes showed curiosity again. "What's your name? I heard 'Meeky.' That is right?"

"You can call me Tim. No, it's Meeker, not Meeky."

"Big fellow with hair on lip, he call you Meeky."

"Yeah," growled Tim. "Well, he isn't right."

"Are you afraid of somethings?"

"No. I don't know."

"Ah, I think not, you who fight bear with hands. Strong spirit."

Molly smiled, pleased with her diagnosis, but she said, "I hear old-timers talk here. They say you are worth four thousand dollars from whose-his-name, Garrey."

Tim stirred uncomfortably. What was going on in this woman's mind? He decided to try diversion.

"How old are you, Molly?"

"Eighteen, I think. I think I was born on July fourth."

"Don't you know?"

"How can I know! Indian don't keep track on dates like white men. The Godmen at mission, they figure about eighteen. How they know that?" She laughed. "I want another beer."

Tim flipped off the cap of a bottle and handed it to her. She took a long drink, and a merry smile lit her face. She moved over to the bed.

Tim put his arms around her, but she stiffened and he withdrew.

"I want an education," said Molly dreamily. "That will be best for me and my people. I will help them."

"I'm sure you will," agreed Tim, whose mind was not on Molly's education. He slid his arm around her waist again, and this time she didn't resist.

"Molly," he whispered, "I like you. You're nice."

The girl sipped her beer and blew at the bubbly foam rising in the neck of the bottle.

Suddenly she thrust away from his arm, facing him squarely. Her dark eyes smoldered.

"That's what you want, ain't it?" she charged, in a complete change of tone and manner. "Just one thing from drunk squaw!"

"Now, Molly . . ."

"I know! Don't tell me, white man. Molly not dumb. You get what you want, you marry me without preacher for one night, and then tomorrow you leave. Then where am I?"

"Molly . . ."

But she was having none of it. She rushed on, her voice rising with indignation.

"You give me baby, huh? And when I have it, where are you? With some white woman, and you don't know me. You walk right past, and I hold kid up for you to see. I saw that happen lots of times. Riverboat men, they stop at our villages and they give girls whiskey. I see lots of half-Indian babies on the Yukon."

As she spoke, her excitement and anger grew until she was shouting.

"You are all bad people!" she cried. "You think Indian is like a dog, you own us. You can do what you want and leave us. We hurt, too. We are not animals."

Enraged, she cocked her arm and threw the bottle against the wall. It crashed and beer spewed around the room. Molly leaped up and threw a bottle again, wild with anger.

"See what booze do, white man?" Tears slid over the high cheeks. "I think I like you, and then find out you are like the others. Oh, damn!"

Again she threw a bottle. The noise brought running foot sounds in the hall. In a moment Frank Leach burst the door open. He stood transfixed, staring first at Molly and then at Tim.

"Well, I'll be danged," he muttered. "Molly, what in the world . . ."

"It's my fault," Tim began, but Molly interrupted.

"I don't need apologies by you," she cried. She whirled on Leach. "I do this myself, and now I quits."

She dashed past the hotel owner and ran down the hall weeping, but as she ran, she shouted, "I going to tell about you, Tim Meeker. You are worth money to me!"

That electrified Tim. Suddenly very sober, he confronted Leach. Leach backed away warily.

"Here now," he said, "I don't know nothing about this. But we don't allow our help to pal around with the guests."

"My fault," said Tim. "Don't fire her."

"If I know Molly" came the reply, "she'll be too ashamed to stay." His eyes narrowed. "Are you the man the law is after?"

Tim put on his coat and stepped around Frank Leach.

"Don't know a thing about it," he said. "Molly is mistaken. Well, see you."

"Hell, man, it's only one ay-em. Where are you going at this hour?"

"I'll find a place." Tim pulled a ten-dollar bill from his wallet. "This will settle for the beer and room. So long."

As he thumped down the steps, doors popped open. He ran out of the hotel and down the trail. His emotions were mixed. He was ashamed of his actions where Molly was concerned, and he was scared.

CHAPTER 8

When Molly dashed from Tim's room, she left the hotel by the rear door and ran behind the bathhouse. There, she stuck her finger down her throat. The finger, having done this work before, performed its duty well, and Molly threw up. When her stomach was emptied, she felt weak and nauseated, but more in control of her mind.

In her heart was a great shame. Twice in the past she had drunk too much. The first experience was at a white man's Christmas party in Tanana. That was three years before, and when liquor was poured into her glass by trappers in town for the holiday, she drank it. It was the first she'd ever tasted and had no idea what its effects would be.

The effects were bad. She lost control of her arms and legs. She staggered and shamed her parents in front of the missionaries, who were present. They were the same Godmen who were her teachers. To make matters even more terrible, several men caught her outdoors when she escaped into the darkness to hide her shame. They tried to take her by force; Molly, drunk or not, wasn't about to give in. She was strong and broke away, fleeing to the safety of the party's bright lights.

A year and a half later, she drank again. This time in a Fort Yukon roadhouse. Her family had stopped at the river town for supplies and an all-night party took place to celebrate the Fourth of July—Molly's birthday, or so it had been decided. There were several women at the party, Indian and white, and they were having "toddies." Molly had never heard of a toddy, so she tried one. It was spicy and delicious, so she tried several more and once again made a fool of herself in front of the crowd, though nobody attempted rape.

From that day, Molly avoided liquor. She was now asking herself why she had drunk with Tim Meeker, him with the blue eyes. Her question was easily answered. She had been attracted to him from the start. Even though she had seen him only briefly at Riley's some five weeks before, she was taken. The bear wounds, his tallness, and the clear honesty in those eyes of the sky, all fascinated Molly. If a man could be beautiful, Tim was beautiful to her. She had by no means forgotten him when he arrived at the Springs. His beard didn't fool her for a minute. She was accustomed to the disguises and ploys of woodland animals. It wasn't by chance that she'd played the record, which began the acquaintance. She wanted to talk, to know the man who fought bears. There was something about him, an air that diminished her wariness of white men. Molly couldn't define what it was—maybe his smile, or the way he carried himself, or, again, the cool eyes that told truth. She couldn't put her feelings into words, nor did she try. Trusting her instincts, she set about establishing lines of communication.

And now it had ended so badly! He was like all the rest, wanting just one thing. Any squaw on the river was good enough for that! Well, she, Molly Jack, was not just any squaw.

As she threw her belongings into a worn packsack, she found that she regretted the outcome. Should she have given in? Would that have hurt? Yes, it would have hurt! But perhaps, at least, she should have not lost her temper. He was in danger from the law, and she'd brought attention to him. That was not good.

Molly thought about this, as she hurried to the front door. She'd been right! He had taken her for an easy one, and what made him think that! Molly's anger flared, and her heart was strong again. No man would ever have her unless she was willing. Not ever! Not even Tim Meeker, the man who fought bears.

Frank Leach met her in the lobby.

"Molly," he said, "I've known you for several years now. You are a good girl, and I'm here to tell you you don't have to leave."

"I know that, Frank," she answered quietly, grateful for the man's sympathy, "but you know I can't be here now. The others, they know me, and I too bashful to see them."

"You mean embarrassed?"

"That is it, I think."

"You are a proud woman, Molly."

"Woman, she has to have something."

"Your family will miss the money you send."

"I will get job in Fairbanks."

Frank Leach sighed and handed Molly a sheaf of greenbacks.

"These are your wages to date."

Molly glanced at the money.

"There is more here than I make."

"Not much, girl. You will need it in town."

"All right, but I pay you back."

She stuck out her hand, and the hotel owner grasped it firmly.

"Things happened too fast here," he said. "I can hardly believe I'm doing this. You always got work here, Molly. Remember that."

The girl nodded, and then did something she had never done in her life—kissed a white man. She touched him lightly on the cheek with her lips, then whirled away, shouldering her packsack.

She left the compound swiftly. Where the trail rounded a bend, she turned to look back. Leach was in the doorway, and she waved. He waved back, then Molly set out in earnest.

Her long legs swung into the measured stride of one accustomed to hiking, and the miles rolled steadily behind. She had no idea of what the Great Spirit, Yako, planned for her in Fairbanks, but she didn't worry. She was, instead, excited. She had never been to a town larger than Fort Yukon. Though an important river port, there were only a few hundred people there, in housing that crowded the riverbank. Except for size, it was like any other Yukon village. The idea of seeing Fairbanks, where she'd heard there were electric lights and steam-heated buildings, thrilled her. People even had outhouses in their homes!

"Yako, guide me," she prayed, speaking in the Kutchin dialect of the Athabascan Indians. "You, all-powerful Shaman of the Tena, take my footsteps, and lead them straight. And may Tsukala, your wife, be at your side. For this, Yako, mighty one, cunning and wise as an old wolf though you may be, needs a woman's understanding."

She tramped on and then spoke again in her tribal dialect.

"And, God, you of the high heaven, you who sent your children to help me learn, I ask for your help, too. I have been told that you help those in need, and, God, I am one."

Molly thought of herself as religious. She was receptive to the mysticism of religion, but she didn't worry over the pros and cons of dogma. She believed there were powers unseen, greater than human powers, and they could, if they wished, destroy or save. Yako, mightiest god of her own people, could work wonders when he wished. She had seen it happen. In a poor fishing year, had not her father knelt before the sky that was Yako's altar and asked for aid? And did not the fish run! Oh, they did! More salmon than ever before. Perhaps Yako did not always answer one's pleas so quickly. Sometimes he didn't seem to hear appeals for help. But he worked in his own way, and in his own time. One did not question Yako. One waited.

Did not the God of white men act in the same baffling manner? Even the missionaries admitted that. God works mysteriously, she had heard them say many times.

Once more, Molly spoke in the Kutchin dialect, addressing God directly.

"I know you will not allow harm to visit so defenseless an Indian girl."

She had to smile a bit at the word "defenseless." Was she that? She who had fought three rapists to a standstill, she who could paddle a flat-bottomed muskrat canoe all day on the marsh lakes of the Yukon country—who could, for that matter, handle canoes on the Yukon itself, with a skill approaching that of her father?

Was she defenseless who once killed a brown bear with her father's .45-90? And who killed a moose every year, except for times of starvation when there were no moose?

Defenseless and weak? Well, perhaps not, but she had one last word.

"Yako, Tsukala, and you, God, you know what I mean. I, Molly Jack, am strong and clever. I can make soup from the wind and clothing from the clouds, but I cannot know what is in cities. I am a girl of the woods. I ask that the way be not bad, that is all."

She finished the journey in three long days, arriving in Fairbanks in late afternoon.

As she approached the town she was afraid. There were people everywhere, more than she had ever seen, even during the greatest of potlatches. There were enough to fill ten villages. Electric lights burned in the stores, even though the sun was shining through the windows. Horse-drawn wagons rocked and rattled through the dusty streets, and the heady racket of massed humanity rose to the sky.

Molly, who could face a grizzly without much fear—there was always some—crossed the Chena Slough on a wooden bridge with much hesitation. As she approached the city proper, her eyes were alive with the sights. So many whites! There were a few brown-skinned people, yes, but they passed her without recognition. It was as if she weren't there. They seemed in a hurry, too, and Molly wondered where they could be going.

In crossing the bridge, she saw the Pioneer Hotel and hurried over. She'd been told this was the place to stay.

She was greeted by the desk clerk, a small man in a white shirt and black string tie. He wore a superior manner as well: when he asked Molly to register, he gazed in surprise when she signed. "Where did you learn to write?" he asked.

"An angel, he showed me!" was the hot retort.

Miffed, the clerk slung a key at her. She snatched it and prowled the hotel's corridors until she found a number on a door that matched the one on her key. It was how it was done, her friends had explained.

She didn't venture out any more that day, but ate apricots and hardtack for supper. She found the indoor outhouse down the hall and was delighted with the contrivance. She flushed the toilet several times just to watch the water disappear and then refill all on its own. Ahhhh-saaaa! That beat anything she'd seen in the woods.

The next few days were harrowing for Molly Jack, late of the Yukon fishing camps. She learned to eat in restaurants and to buy from women clerks in the stores. She was abashed by their loud voices and uncaring eyes. Indian women did not speak so loudly, except when they were women alone, no men around.

She was surprised to see white men unloading firewood at the town's power plant. Where she was from, the women brought in the wood, so men would be free to hunt and fish. Hunting and fishing were the basis of life. Successful hunters fed the village, and without them, hunger followed. It was a simple equation, one Molly learned young.

But if she was fascinated by what she was seeing, she accepted it. She was, as well she knew, in a world dominated by white skins. And, exceptions not denied, most were her enemies. Her one purpose in being in Fairbanks was not to see the town itself, and certainly not its people. She was going to use the town as a stepping-stone to bigger things—more important matters. She wanted an education, and that meant Seattle, for it was there the schools were. To get to that far place one needed money. The job at Leach's had gone sour. Very well. But there must be other jobs in this white man's town. Lots of them.

She hunted for work during the day, and in the evening she roamed the streets, curious. What was life like here? She had seen Indians—what did they do?

Her tours were confined mainly to the downtown area, and what she saw she didn't like. Native people were in the bars with the whites. Native men drank too much and traded their ancient wilderness dignity for loose smiles, wobbly legs, and silly laughter. Nor were the women any better. They were worse, because they left with white men and did not return. Or if they did, they came back alone, their dresses rumpled. Molly didn't need a diagram to tell her what was happening.

But even these things she absorbed. She accepted them, because there was nothing she could do about them. Not now. Maybe some day, when she knew more, when she had an education, the knowledge would lead her to a solution of such shameful matters.

Nor did she dare pause in front of the taverns for long, because there were offers from any number of men, some of them Indians! If she were a drinker, she could have remained drunk for a long time, maybe months, maybe years. How many native women had already done that! She was thankful now for the hard lessons about liquor she had had. They taught her caution.

After several days of job hunting, Molly found her money running low. The snippy hotel clerk demanded each day's rent in advance, and restaurant food was high. Frank Leach had tucked a tidy extra sum among the greenbacks, but Molly's purse was nearly flat.

On the fourth day, in late afternoon, she stopped in the Palace Bathhouse and Hotel, Canna Phipps, Proprietor. It was a small log building on Fourth Avenue, just off the main street.

The owner, a middle-aged lady from the Deep South, measured Molly's physique with a shrewd eye.

"You're what I'm lookin' for, girl. This is a small place, sure, but I got baths to clean in addition to bed makin' and all that. Can you handle it?"

Molly could have dressed a whale in a sailor suit, if it meant wages, and she nodded quickly.

"The pay is seventy-five a month," said her new employer, "and you have your own room. You can cook, too, on a hot plate. Just don't smell the place up."

Molly checked out of the Pioneer Hotel with a flourish. She slung the key at the clerk, just the same as he'd slung it at her. As she stomped out, she heard him mutter, "Stupid squaw!"

She very nearly went back to punch him one, but she controlled her temper and stamped over to the Palace.

When Canna Phipps saw her face, she asked, "You been in a fight, honey?"

"No! But I like to be!"

"Who with?"

Molly told her about the hotel clerk.

Canna put an arm around Molly's shoulder and said, "Don't worry about him, girl. There are lots like him in the world, and they are nothin', see? If you worry about them, you are wastin' your time, because you are worryin' about nothin'. Do you see what I'm gettin' at?"

"Yeah. I guess I know."

"Sure you do. Now put your things away and come eat with me. I fixed enough stew to feed all Fairbanks, and you're welcome to have some."

That night Molly did some figuring. The seventy-five-a-month salary was good for the kind of work she did. But it wasn't going to be enough to get her to school, not even if she saved for a year. At the Springs she had no expenses; both food and room were furnished. But town living was expensive. She needed more clothes—a new dress anyway. The old one she wore at the Springs wouldn't do now.

She was grateful for the job, but at the same time she was discouraged. She wanted her education to begin now, not in five years; not even in two years, but now. She was impatient with waiting any longer, for she had planned this since she was a child. She would simply have to get another job. She would work eighteen hours a day if necessary. It would be easy. She had been on winter trapline trails for longer than that. Eighteen hours—that was nothing.

She would find another job tomorrow.

CHAPTER 9

Stumping over the return trail to Riley's, Tim cussed himself up one side and down the other, inside and out. Why had he acted like a fool? He'd never done such an idiot thing in his life, so why now? He might just as well have stood naked on a chair in front of the hotel, and hollered for everybody to come see. That couldn't have brought more attention than Molly running from him, while yelling that he was worth a whole pile of money. Just what he didn't need—the spotlight.

More than one white man had slept with an Indian woman, and there hadn't been a revolution about it. After all, the feelings between a man and a woman didn't halt at the color line. But *he* managed to pick the only one in fifty miles who looked as if she could break his head. She was crazy that one, Molly Jack.

But Tim couldn't dismiss his own behavior that easily. He felt bad. He liked Molly Jack. There was something about her that appealed to him. An honesty, maybe, or her toughness. And she hadn't been at all hostile at first. She liked him, or, at least, she liked the "bear killer." It was just his rotten luck that the affair went sour. You could kiss a cherub sometimes and catch on fire or kick the devil and lose your wings.

Riley was putting on the morning coffee when he arrived.

The old man was suspicious.

"Only critters I see traveling this early are robins and robbers. What went wrong?"

Tim ignored the sarcasm, asking, "Did an Indian girl stop here?" There was just a chance.

Riley shook his head and growled, "Good grief, you ain't in trouble that way are you?"

"Not anymore. Sure you didn't see her?"

"I'd have told you yes if I did," was the testy response. "Listen, I told you not to go for play-play."

Tim lapsed into a defensive silence.

Riley softened after the first cup of coffee melted the anger knots in his stomach.

"Hell," he muttered, "I don't know why I'm so hard on you, boy. What you do is your own business."

"Not altogether."

"Meaning?"

"I owe you a lot, Riley."

"Yeah, well, I don't want you to land in the calaboose. Like I said before, I think you ought to be clearin' your name."

"Right."

"Soon, Tim. You can't hide forever."

"Give this beard another week, then I'll go to Fairbanks."

Riley agreed and seemed relieved to have heard a positive statement.

"I like that," he said. "What's the plan?"

"I'll look for a paper trail, meaning Garrett's records of his underhanded deals. If I find it, I can set a trap that will get him for sure."

"Sounds good."

"Better be. It's all I've got."

On the way to Jake's cabin with Buck under him, Tim mulled over recent events and came to the conclusion that he'd better act soon. The longer Garrett had to cook up more lies, the worse off Tim would be. And there was no doubt in his mind that Garrett and Hendrickson would connive. It's what they were good at.

For the next several days Tim left the cabin early and deliberately remained away until late. It was very possible that there were those at the Springs who, guessing he was the one worth four thousand, would try tracking him down. After a week and no bounty hunters appeared, he felt easier.

One evening, after an all-day sortie, he returned with a full plan of action. He'd go to Garrett's office, *his* office, and search. Someplace there had to be records, and the office was the most likely place to start. If he found nothing, then he'd try Garrett's home and then Ruth's place. By elimination, he'd narrow possibilities until he struck pay dirt.

But when he opened the door of Jake's cabin, he met Deputy Marshal Dwyer face to face. Dwyer held a .30-30 carbine, and it was pointing straight at Tim's gut.

"Welcome," said the lawman. "And please don't try anything ridiculous this time."

The sight of Dwyer was a shock. Tim gaped. Neither man spoke for a moment, as Tim slowly absorbed the importance of what was happening.

"You knew I was here all the time, didn't you?" he asked finally.

Dwyer nodded. "I knew you were in the area, but not exactly where. In between other jobs, I been hunting, and, lo! here you are." Dwyer glanced around. "Place belongs to Jake Lindstrum, judging by letters he got and like that."

"He had no idea I was here."

"Oh, I bet not!" The deputy was very happy. "But I don't care about him, bucko. I'd have a time proving he did know, and it ain't important, anyhow. You are the one I want, and I got Y-O-U!"

"Did you see me at Riley's?"

"How could I miss? You were right at my feet."

"Why didn't you take me then?"

"And cut the whole sweet pie into so many pieces? No, no, my friend. I want the entire delicious thing."

"Garrett's bounty, of course."

"Of course."

Dwyer motioned with his rifle.

"Saddle up. My nag is hid uptrail. I'll ride yours that far. We'll use your trail to Central. Yeah," he grinned, "I found it. And then it's Circle for us."

Things were going mightily wrong for Mrs. Meeker's son, thought Tim angrily. He should have known Dwyer had seen him. A man whose training and experience prepared him for just such events could hardly miss.

After throwing a saddle on Buck, Tim led off on foot, while Dwyer rode behind.

"You know," observed the lawman, "I could get your friend Riley too. No reward in it, but helping a criminal is against the law."

"I'm no criminal," muttered Tim. "Nothing has been proven."

But he was worried. He didn't want to see any of his friends in trouble because of him.

"Listen," he called over his shoulder, "doesn't my saving your life in Birch Creek have any meaning?"

"Sure does, and I thank you."

"Real gratitude would do more than say thanks."

"Like what?"

"Let me go. I'm innocent, Dwyer. I've been set up by my partner, Garrett, and," Tim hesitated, "by my former fiancée, Ruth Claxton."

"I don't doubt it" was the hearty response. "What I've seen of Garrett, he's a snake. Don't know anything about your lady, but if she's in cahoots with Garrett, I believe she could set you up all right."

"If I go to jail, I'll never be able to prove my innocence."

"That's your problem" came the curt reply. "All's I know is what the law tells me. And it tells me you are guilty as sin."

"Then, listen, leave Riley alone. He didn't do much. We're longtime friends, and he could hardly turn me in. You'd do as much, Dwyer."

Tim could almost hear the wheels in the man's think box

grinding. Finally, the deputy said, very reluctantly, "Well, I got nothing against the old man. It's you I want, and it's you I got."

Plus four thousand dollars, thought the outlaw in despair.

They plunged through the tunnel of willows, twigs snapping and whipping. Tim heard Dwyer cuss and slap back. If the man had any sense, he'd walk. At that moment, the deputy let out a string of red-hot oaths that would have made a Fairbanks prostitute harken, and saddle leather creaked. Tim glanced behind and caught Dwyer swinging from saddle to ground and for that instant off guard.

Tim acted swiftly, barging into his captor, knocking him to the ground. At the same time, he grabbed the carbine and wrenched it from an iron grip. In a few seconds the tables were reversed. Tim was in command, and Dwyer, gazing down the same gun barrel that had been an ally such a short time before, knew it. His language was enriched by the experience, and the air was blue with invective.

"That kind of talk never made the teacher smile," said Tim happily. "Now, Mr. Deputy Marshal Dwyer, bounty hunter, as it were, get next to that fat spruce yonder."

"God damn you!" exploded the captive in a fury. "I'll track you down if it's the last thing I ever do."

"You mean, you'll track down the four thousand. Well, I got news for you. I'm going to settle this in the next few days or go to jail. You won't see me again, Dwyer."

Tim wrapped the deputy's arms around the bole of the tree so that his back was tight against the rough bark. Then he tied the unfortunate man's wrists together, using the leather thongs from Dwyer's own boots. He threw the boots into the river.

"If you get loose before I am way far away," he explained, "I want you to be mighty careful not to break your toesies on the rocks, stumps, and snags. Walk slow, old fellow."

Dwyer snarled.

"It's what you get for cheating your associates," said Tim,

very pleased with how things had turned out. "You should always be honest, man of law. And now, so long."

"Hey!" shouted Dwyer in sudden panic. "How am I going to get loose? The skeeters will eat me alive."

There were already swarms zeroing in.

"Maybe a bear will get you first," said Tim, feeling mean. "See you—maybe."

Clutching the carbine, Tim mounted Buck, and suffering the willows, rode through them with averted face. He found Dwyer's horse and arrived at Central with him in tow.

When they arrived, Riley stared.

"Now what . . . ," he began, but Tim interrupted, explaining the situation in quick monosyllables, as time was of the essence.

"In about six hours," he finished, "go let Dwyer loose. He'll love you for it, I'm sure. In the meantime, I've tracks to make, and I need grub."

Riley filled Tim's saddlebags without delay. He added a blanket and a trap, then handed Tim a box of .30-30 ammunition.

Tim refused the cartridges.

"No firearms," he decided. "There's not going to be any shooting. Give the carbine back to Dwyer. I don't want it said I robbed the law. Got any stove blacking?"

Riley rummaged in a cupboard and handed Tim a box.

"Now why that?" the old-timer asked.

"To fix my beard."

Tim swung into the saddle, but leaned down and grasped Riley's hand.

"You've been a true and loyal friend, Riley, and I won't forget that. I know I've been a pain, but I'm innocent. I'm hoping that your trouble won't have been for nothing."

Then he was off, and the trail sped behind under Buck's hoofs. Tim was aware of the fact that no matter how fast he traveled, a telegram would beat him to Fairbanks. Dwyer would give a complete description of him, including the beard.

That's where the blacking would come into use. He left Central with a red beard, but would arrive in town with a black one.

Urging Buck to his best effort, without wearing the horse out, Tim made it to Fairbanks in slightly under forty-eight hours. Under cover of a thick patch of forest on the outskirts of town, he switched from a red to a black beard. It was a messy job and wouldn't last, but he hoped it would last long enough. He added Riley's dark glasses, and hunching down in his mackinaw, entered town.

As a test, he put Buck up in the Pioneer Hostelries. The owner, a man Tim knew, never moved so much as an eyebrow in recognition. Satisfied, Tim sat at the counter in the Model Cafe for coffee. Tom Yule, who had given Ruth her first job, was affable and did allow himself an overtime glance at the beard. He'd never seen one quite so black, but, to Tim's relief, he turned to other customers without so much as another look.

Out of curiosity, Tim strolled past the Aurora Tavern. The customers were lined up at the bar, the tables full. Apparently, the place was doing better than ever, and Tim succumbed to a heated wave of rebellion. Why was he sneaking around? He ought to charge in there right now, yelling his head off that, by damn, he was not guilty of anything! *Nothing!*

The temptation was so strong that for a moment Tim felt his muscles tighten, ready to spring into action. But the saving balm of common sense diverted the impulse, and Tim walked away quickly. It had been close. He went to a hardware store and purchased a small crowbar. Chances were, his keys still fit the doors, but if not, he had the tool that would open them.

Time passed slowly. There was nothing he could do until after the bar closed at two in the morning. Meanwhile he meandered around town. He decided against going to Jake's place. Could be that it was being watched, and he'd already caused his friend enough trouble.

Once, in passing the Aurora, he saw Garrett and Ruth. They were having a drink, and Garrett still hunched toward her in his aggressive manner. To his surprise, Tim found that his feelings for Ruth were indifferent. The woman who had once stirred deep emotions left him without any feeling at all. But he had the wisdom to realize that was not probably true of Ruth. She was dangerous. She'd turn him into a jailbird with no more compunction than it would take to step on a cockroach.

Even knowing that, Tim could muster no indignation over Ruth, but seeing Garrett was another matter and he hurried away. His emotions told him flatly that he feared Garrett. The man's arrogance and brutish strength were super bogeys in his mind. On the evening that he'd challenged Garrett and had, in fact, broken the man's jaw, he had yielded to an inspired, jealous rage. He'd have struck a bronze statue, fought a dozen bears, taken San Juan Hill single-handed that night.

But that night was gone forever, and with it his courage. He no longer felt a passion for Ruth. That inspiring force had vanished. It came down, now, to just Garrett and himself, and he wasn't ready to face his former partner. He was still "Meeky" insofar as Garrett was concerned.

Such thoughts laid Tim's morale low. He felt dirty and negative, and his spirits sank. Doubt kicked at him—could he find any incriminating records? They were his only chance. And if he did find any, would he have the courage to use them?

Discouraged, he headed for the Palace Bathhouse. He needed a good soaking and maybe he could cleanse away some of the grunge that sludged up his mind. What should have been an exciting and positive time for him had charted a reverse course. He had never felt worse.

CHAPTER 10

Tim knew Canna Phipps slightly. In order to increase the effectiveness of what he realized was not the best disguise in the world, he averted his head slightly and mumbled when he spoke. He was led to a tub without undue passage of speech, for which he was thankful.

Once in the tub, Tim relaxed. As he soaked neck deep, the tension that had been abuilding since his arrival in town dissolved somewhat.

There were some newspapers on a nearby stool, and Tim glanced through them.

The Blue Parka bandit had kept his reputation intact by robbing the cleanup at Number Three above Discovery claim on Cleary Creek. He made a successful getaway with dust valued at fifteen thousand dollars. There was a reward of two thousand for his capture.

Another robbery took place at Number Four above Discovery on Dome Creek. This robber held three miners at pistol point, took their cash and all the gold. Altogether, he harvested five thousand. There was a reward of one thousand dollars for him.

Tim found it almost funny that he was high in the same league. The four thousand offered for him wasn't exactly penny ante.

The Tanana Valley Mines Railroad was planning an extension toward Circle City from Chatanika, the present northern terminus. Falcon Joslyn, president of the line, claimed it could be done. He should know, for he'd long been interested in railroad matters in Alaska.

Gordon's Dry Goods was having a women's wear sale. Tim made a face. He could just see Ruth in the thick of it. Would Molly Jack take advantage of the sale if she were in town? Chances were, she didn't know what a sale was.

As he turned the pages, learning what familiar names were doing, Tim's spirits dropped again. He, too, had once been part of a new town growing. He had served on committees, helping decide what would be best for the community now and in the future. He'd even made speeches, and he'd enjoyed it all. It had been exciting and he wanted his town to prosper. Fairbanks, so went the feeling, would amount to more than just another mining camp. It would become a permanent city. Since leaving the mountainous coast of southeastern Alaska, Tim had grown to love the interior. Fairbanks was home.

He had come to know prominent men such as Falcon Joslyn, and Judge James Wickersham. Wickersham was the Territory's present delegate to Congress and a power in the land. Many thought that as goes the judge, so goes Alaska.

And he knew men like lawyer John Clark, who had bicycled to Fairbanks over the Valdez Trail in midwinter 1906. He had shared lunch many times with Sam Bonnifield, president of the First National Bank, a man who followed the mining game closely. Yes, he'd even traded political insights with Governor Will Hoggatt when the latter was touring Alaska!

Hell, he'd met them all, the high and the low, if, in Alaska, there was a low. Frontier living pretty much equalized everybody. The scarcity of people drew them closer together. The mucker said howdy to the bank president and received a howdy in return.

Was that all gone for him now? It had been a high-stakes game, and he liked it. He was good at it. Though he didn't see himself as a "climber," he enjoyed being a member of the inner circle.

Tim flung the newspaper on the floor, and a boxed announcement flung itself back at him:

Mr. Michael Garrett and Miss Ruth Claxton announced their engagement at a gathering of close friends last evening. Mr. Garrett is a prominent businessman and a leader in civic affairs. Miss Claxton, a citizen of our community for two years, is an associate of Mr. Garrett. No date has been set for the wedding, but Mr. Garrett admitted with a smile, "Soon."

So it was happening. Tim almost laughed, though there was little humor in his thinking. If ever a pair deserved each other, it was those two. Both were as sly as foxes.

Tim remained in the bath until his fingers wrinkled from the water, then he dressed, and stepped into the night. There were still two hours to kill, before he could try his scheme.

He wandered the back streets, his emotions blowing hot and cold. Was he being a fool? Should he pull out and go back to Central? What did he stand to gain, actually, if he found incriminating records? On the other hand, what choice was there?

At one point, he turned toward Jake's place. Maybe Jake would have some ideas. But he turned about again, after a block or two, determined to keep his resolve. Leave Jake out of it. This was Tim Meeker's fight.

After what seemed a very long time—a hellish time, in fact—the clock registered 2 A.M. He checked the Aurora from across the street and found the place dark. The customers had gone. Now was the time for action.

He circled around to the rear of the building and tried his key. The lock yielded quietly, and Tim ducked inside. So far, so good. Apparently, the fire hadn't damaged the doors.

It was shadowy, but he climbed the rebuilt stairs without hesitation. He'd climbed them often enough in what was beginning to seem like a long time ago.

He tried the office key, and the door swung open easily.

Easy! Things were going well. Perhaps too well? He entered the room with tingling nerves and walked straight into the leveled pistol of Sike Hendrickson.

"Greetings," said Hendrickson, with a huge smile.

Tim froze.

There were others in the room. Shadows moved and a lamp was lit, revealing Garrett and Molly Jack.

Tim stared at the girl, then said, "Molly, did you do this?"

"Sure she did!" interrupted Garrett. "She's a smart squaw and knows how easy it is to make a little money."

"But where . . . ," began Tim.

"At Palace," said Molly. "I works there."

Garrett cut in.

"We wanted to make sure we got the right man, Meeky, so we asked Molly to come along. Kind of figured you'd visit here." He nodded to Hendrickson, "All right, let's get it over with."

In the gloom, Tim heard Sike's pistol double cock. At the same instant, Molly cried out, "No, not that. You promise me not to kill him."

"We caught him robbing my office," growled Garrett. "What you waiting for, Sike?"

Molly's interruption gave Tim time to understand that he was a dead man if he didn't do something. He dove to one side, as the pistol roared. The slug slammed into his shoulder, knocking him flat, but his mind was clear, never more clear in his life. He saw the tableau in perfect, instant relief: Sike was in front of him, Garrett to the right, Molly to the left. And in that moment he felt no fear. He knew exactly what must be done.

He came up with a dive at Hendrickson's middle, knocking the would-be killer down, but not before another shot deafened him from inches away.

Leaping clear, Tim ran. He hurled down the steps three at a time and raced through the alley.

Garrett and Hendrickson thumped after him, Hendrickson's

six-shooter bucking all the while. Tim steeled himself, waiting for a bullet to tear into his body. He zigzagged, making as difficult a target as possible. He rounded the corner and was speeding toward the main street when he was abruptly halted by the barrel of another pistol. This one was clutched in the firm hand of Deputy Marshal Tod Cowles.

"Well," said the deputy, "if it isn't our flown pigeon."

Tim was beginning to feel his shoulder wound. He swayed, as his senses began to fold.

"All crimes should be committed across the street from the marshal's office," said Cowles. "They practically solve themselves. Give me your weapon."

"Don't have one."

"Who did the shooting?"

"Them," replied Tim, as Garrett and Hendrickson came to an angry-faced stop.

Sike raised his pistol, crying, "One more shot and that skinny punk will cause no more problems."

"Pull that trigger, Sike," suggested Cowles in a tight voice, "and I'll sing at your funeral."

"He was robbing us," hissed Sike. "He shot at us."

"Don't see any gun on him," Cowles observed calmly. "Let your piece down, *now!*"

The man still hesitated. There was a wild fire in his pale eyes, an intense eagerness. That eagerness is to see my dead body, thought Tim. The man enjoys killing, and he doesn't like being disappointed.

"Sike," prompted Garrett, "let it go."

Hendrickson slowly holstered his gun, but the wildness never left his eyes.

"Let's go!" thundered Garrett. "Nothing more we can do here. Deputy Cowles has everything under control." As he and Sike turned away, Garrett added, "See you in court, Meeky. You'll get five to ten for this." He grinned wickedly. "That's almost as good as seeing you dead."

As Tim was crossing the street with Cowles, he saw Molly. She was watching from a distance.

"Thanks, Molly!" he called. "Have a happy education!" He suspected even at that terrible moment why she'd turned him over to Garrett.

The girl whirled away, running in the direction of the Palace. Tim wasn't sure, but in the still morning air, he thought he heard her weeping. A little late to be sorry, he muttered, a little late.

Cowles called a doctor to tend Tim's wound, and after the medic left, the deputy said, "You're going to need a lawyer. Know one?"

"I can get John Clark. He's done some business for me."

"All right. Call him in the morning." Cowles looked at Tim shrewdly. "How," he asked, "did you ever get mixed up in a thing like this? I always knew you to be pretty level-headed."

"It's a cooked-up deal," replied Tim. "Garrett's behind the whole thing."

"I thought you were friends, as well as partners."

"So did I."

The deputy nodded.

"Well, it's not for me to disbelieve you," came the surprising statement. "Anybody who hires Sike Hendrickson isn't all that good." He frowned. "But it will be up to the judge what happens. You know that."

Tim nodded, and then, feeling weak and very weary, he lay down on his cell cot and slept.

CHAPTER 11

The judge sentenced Tim to three hundred and sixty-four days in the Fairbanks courthouse jail. Tim was mortified. He had thought he'd be sent Outside to a federal prison, possibly McNeil Island in Washington. To be incarcerated so close to those whom he knew was something he did not want. The humiliation of receiving a sentence at all was bad enough.

He protested the sentence through his attorney, John Clark. The judge, accustomed to a frontier breed, had seen peculiar things. One new ward of the government had cut off his thumb in protest. Another had vomited to show how he felt. But to request a longer sentence?

"You understand," he said to Tim, "that if I send you to McNeil, the sentence will have to be longer than a year—say, a year and a day. You'll get two more days out of it."

Clark and Tim talked it over. Tim asked if the judge was having some fun and Clark assured him that, no, the judge was dead serious. So Tim dropped the matter, already asinine enough.

As far as he was concerned, the trial had been a complete farce. Though Clark had competently brought in many witnesses who swore to Tim's unblemished character, it wasn't enough. Garrett was able to produce many eyewitnesses. They all swore that Meeker had set fire to the Aurora Tavern deliberately, had robbed the till at gunpoint, had bashed Ruth Claxton, and had broken Mr. Garrett's jaw. It was open and shut. The judge had no choice.

"Be patient," advised Clark. "You'll probably get out in April or May, with time off for good behavior."

This news and advice failed to impress Tim. A bitterness that was already seeded found an enriched soil and grew rapidly. He found that he couldn't take his fate philosophically. He had been royally flimflammed by his former friend and partner, by Ruth his onetime sweetheart, and by the law itself. Where was that fairness the courts bragged about? Anybody, even a mossy-backed judge, would know that he, Timothy Meeker, could not possibly have done all he was charged with. Hell, he had too much to lose! As an avid booster of Fairbanks, why would he do such a stupid thing as burn his own place of business!

But in the end he went sullenly to his new home, cell 001. The main boarders in the local calaboose, Tim learned, were drunks. They were fellows, young and old, who worked during the summer, but by the end of October had invested all their money in whiskey. They then committed some minor crime and were indicted for vagrancy and received a six-month term in the pen. There was a subtle agreement between the drunks and the law that such a punishment would be pronounced. Many of the drunks returned every fall, content in the knowledge that winter's stunning fifty below would not find them. It was warm in jail.

Two things happened to Tim in prison that would remain with him for the rest of his life. The first of these was meeting Mickey Jenderson, a drunk. He was about Tim's age, a cheery sort of a man, who easily admitted that he was equally at home in the calaboose and the miner's bunkhouse. He grew a thick red beard that resembled Tim's, before Tim shaved his off. He had come to detest it. It itched and collected dirt. If he didn't wash it every day, it stank.

Tim, whose sole visitors had been a few friends, John Clark, and Jake Lindstrum, was glad when Mickey became his cellmate.

"I know you," declared the newcomer, "see you a lot in the Aurora."

"I own half of it."

"What are you doing here?"

Tim, eager for talk of any kind, poured out his story, all of it. At the end, Mickey clucked his tongue in sympathy.

"I know that Garrett gent," he said. "He's a mean one. Him and Sike are a dandy pair. Leave it to them, and Fairbanks would become one big outhouse." He scanned Tim's features. "Hell, you ain't like them. I can tell by your face. Faces always tell about a man. Honest people get fooled by crooks pretty easily."

"Well, this one did, all right."

"How about the squaw?"

Tim hated the word "squaw" and said as much. As far as he was concerned it was derogatory. An Indian never used the term, only whites.

Mickey grinned. "Ah, pardon me, no offense meant. Tell me about her. She plunked you in the clink, yet you don't hold a grudge?"

"If it hadn't been her, it would have been somebody else—probably Dwyer. I'd just as soon she got the money."

"I think you have more than a financial interest in her."

"Well," Tim plumbed the depths quickly and found his feelings for Molly substantial. "I think she's the one I'm going to marry."

Mickey's face lit up. "Well, I'll be . . ."

Tim nodded, amused and surprised by his own statement. "Just thought of that myself."

"Yeah, I can see that. Well, a lot of men marry Indians—and they get good wives."

Tim appraised his new acquaintance. "What about yourself, what are you doing in here?"

"It don't matter where you live," declared the man, "as long as it satisfies you."

"You like this?"

"Beats hell out of a fifty-below nest under the Chena Slough bridge."

"Bridge?"

Mickey Jenderson threw back his head and laughed.

"Hey, fella, here you are a prominent citizen of this burg . . ."

"Was," prompted Tim.

"All right, was, and you don't know about the bridge? I spent many a night there, summer and winter. The deputies don't bother us. As long as we're out of sight, we're out of mind."

"So if you don't make it here for the winter, you camp under the bridge."

"Sure! You get a good fire going, and it ain't bad. But this is better."

The man's bright outlook on the grimmer aspects of life—such as bare survival—attracted Tim. If it hadn't been for the Happy Swede, as Tim called him, jail would have been much lonelier.

One day he asked, "Why don't you get out of this rut?"

"Rut?"

"You could do something with your life. You're smart. How come you're wasting around like you are?"

Mickey shrugged. "Can't really say. Just drifted into this style of living, I guess, but I don't think I'm a born drunk, either. I don't know."

"You ought to find out."

"Yeah, well, I have decided to do something about John Barleycorn. It's booze that brings me here. I'm a drunkard and know it. But I been thinking about tapering off." He held up a hand, when Tim started to speak. "Just thinking, mind you. Whiskey brings a lot of comfort." He laughed at Tim's surprised look. "Sure it does! Why do you think there are drunks?"

Tim, not being a proselytizer for the advantages of sobriety or anything else, let the subject drop. He liked Mickey, though, and, proselytizer or not, intended to pick it up again, when the time was more favorable.

Eventually seven more men found winter lodgings in the Fairbanks jail. Tim knew some of them as customers at the Aurora, when they were in the money. He'd sometimes wondered where they'd disappeared to and now he knew.

But there were no women.

"They send women Outside," explained Mickey. "Guess they don't like co-ed clinks. Too bad." The Happy Swede grinned. "Could use one or two, you know?"

The guards were a friendly bunch. They knew most of the prisoners in and out of jail. There were no cruelties, no harassment or tensions between outlaws and inlaws, as Mickey put it.

Inexperienced though he was, Tim realized that probably few houses of detention were as lenient. However, as Mickey pointed out, try and walk away and see what happens. In spite of the relative ease of the life, Tim came to resent the walls and bars, and even the good-natured guards. The bastards could leave at night for home and hearth, and that freedom galled Tim. He knew he was wrong in his feelings, but he couldn't help it. He couldn't leave when he wanted to, at the end of a shift, and that reminded him, day after day, as much as anything, that he was in *prison*.

An event he dreaded was the weekly work party. Under the supervision of an old-timer called Pop, a guard, the inmates cleaned the downtown streets of the city. Tim had seen these crews often in his free days, but had paid little attention. It was just something the city did to get free labor. But now, on the other side of the bars, he saw the matter in a wholly different light. It was torture to be pushing a broom and see those on the outside with whom he'd shared a drink or a laugh. Some said hello, but most turned their heads and hurried on, embarrassed.

Garrett and Ruth passed occasionally, ignoring him. Sike Hendrickson occasionally watched him from afar. Still sulking because he missed his target in the office, thought Tim wryly. And, most probably, planning how to correct a botched job.

The sum total of the work parties left him feeling degraded. In spite of his efforts to talk himself out of a declining mood, his bitterness increased. Though not guilty of anything except choosing a bad partner, he began to feel criminal by inference. As the months passed, his morale and his opinion of himself dropped to a dreary low.

Though most of the prisoners were drunks, he learned that there were also prisoners of a more deadly kind.

During the course of winter two hard-looking robbers and a murderer were guests of the governor.

The first two had beaten their victim senseless and fled to Dawson, in Canada. They were apprehended by the Canadian Royal Northwest Mounted Police and handed back to Alaskan authorities. Eventually, they received ten-year sentences and were sent Outside.

The murderer had killed his prospecting partner in a lonely cabin on the Tolovana River. Meeting him was the second thing in Tim's prison life to create a lasting impression.

The man was cold-blooded. As Mickey pointed out, he had no more feelings for humanity than a starving polar bear.

"He had his killin' comin' to him," claimed the man of his partner. "He was always s' good, yuh know? Packing that damned Bible everywheres!"

After his trial brought a conviction of first-degree murder and a hanging sentence, he confessed to more killings.

"I done away with three others of those bastards, too. They all had it comin'. S' good, yuh know? Wouldn't hurt the nose on a fly. Well, I showed 'em. Yessir, they's quiet now."

He laughed often and loud, a crazy loon's gargle that gave Tim the shivers. The man bragged about his crimes, claiming he'd done the world a favor and ought to get a medal instead of a necktie party. He called the U.S. marshals a flock of fatheads for not catching him before. And all of his talk was punctuated by his crazy loon's laugh.

The day he was hanged was also an outside workday for the prisoners. For once, Tim looked forward to it, but the detail was cancelled. The guards were uneasy. Even though none of the inmates would have tried to escape—where would they go in wintertime Alaska?—poor morale made them a bad risk. There could be a fight, or maybe they'd give Pop a hard time. Low morale brought problems.

Though the killer deserved his fate, everybody agreed, the prisoners had come to know him at close quarters. If there was no sorrow over his execution, there was sorrow that they'd ever met the man at all. He had created a harrowing impression, and when he was led off to the gallows, they watched in glum apathy.

The hanging took place at ten in the morning in a room not far from the cellblock. To his everlasting horror, Tim felt the wooden building shake as the killer danced his way to oblivion. He developed a depression beyond all words. The world was for a few days a dark hell. Even Mickey Jenderson was affected and lapsed into a moody silence.

In April, Tim was released, with time off for good behavior, as John Clark had predicted. Though it was a vast relief to be freed of government shackles, Tim's soul had become shadowed. If there was a light in that most intimate of human recesses, he reckoned it burned with a black light.

Mickey Jenderson was let out at the same time.

"Don't let it get you," he advised. "It ain't always so great being in jail. Awful things do happen, but you can't let it get you."

Tim agreed, but the advice was lost on him.

The loyal Jake had come to meet him, and the two returned to his cabin. Tim promptly drank more than his share of a quart.

Just before a welcome darkness, he muttered, "I thought getting out of jail would be a happy time. But it isn't. It isn't at all."

CHAPTER 12

The man who had created such miserable changes in Tim Meeker's life was finishing a speech. The audience leaned forward, pleased by what it saw and heard.

Garrett was tall and broad-shouldered. His tailored suit fit in such a manner as to suggest great physical power. Strength was an appreciated attribute in a land where most of the male population earned their living with their hands.

Garrett was proud of his nose. He had once studied the early Greeks in a high school history class. The textbook had been illustrated with Grecian scenes, including photos of Greek statues. He thought his nose, though a trifle large, was patterned along the lines of Apollo, god of sunlight.

The eyes of the speaker were dark and observant. Some would say watchful. They pierced the world aggressively, from under bushy, jetblack brows. His lips were generous in width, but lacking in substance. They formed two thin, bloodless lines, the most unpromising feature in an otherwise manly, forthright visage. But the lips were kept hidden under the moustache, much as a copse of trees will shield an ugly hillside gash.

The chamber of commerce, gathered for its monthly luncheon, paid heed as Garrett spoke. In fact, they listened with an acuteness usually reserved for governors, congressional delegates, and rich mining men. Garrett, if not rich, was getting there; if not governor, had not laughed when a suggestion was made that he'd be a good one. He was already mayor of Fairbanks, the Golden Heart. The town was one of the richest centers in Alaska and a likely stepping-stone to higher political office. When Fairbanks spoke, even those in distant Washington, D.C., cupped an ear.

"We are a growing community," said the mayor in conclusion. "Nay, I would say wealthy. Some of the best mining ground in the world lies within a day's hike *in any direction!* The words 'Golden Heart' were not coined haphazardly. They mean just what they say."

Applause, prolonged and earnest.

"In another year," the voice concluded, a voice of deep and pleasing timbre, "our little town, our *metropolis,* will be the focal point of the entire northwest or my name isn't Michael Garrett, *and we must be ready!"*

Shouts of approval, as the chamber rose, luncheon over. Single file, like a millipede of many legs, the chamber passed by Garrett, agreeing, congratulating, promising. In the end, he was left alone. That was just what he wanted.

He allowed his gaze to wander among the empty tables. Waiters were clearing the dishes, but Garrett ignored them. He leaned back in his chair and lit a thin cigar, drawing the smoke with keen satisfaction. He examined the cigar approvingly. Genuine Cuban tobacco, an import that only he and a few others could afford.

His speech had gone well, he thought. That phrase about getting to the mines by hiking had been a good one. Though he, himself, always rode a good horse, the word "hiking" gave the matter a common touch. His speech would be printed in the *Times,* and the men on the creeks would read that. Damn few of them owned horses.

He was well liked, of that he was certain. The puppy eyes of the diners told him that Mike Garrett was their man of the hour. Their unabashed admiration was unmistakable, and, like puppies, he had them eating out of his hand. A few more contributions to worthy causes, and—who knew? William Howard Taft was President, and he had donated heavily to the Republican party. He had talked to Wickersham, the delegate to

Congress, but the results were vague. Well, if Wickersham didn't approve him, there were other ways to gain the attention of the mighty. He reached into his vest pocket and withdrew a twenty-dollar bill. Yes, there were other avenues to power.

The bowie-knife moustache, combed and tamed for its public appearance, curled upward, giving expression to the thin smile beneath. A small smile, perhaps, but weighted with significance. Garrett was in a triumphant upswing of life, and things were getting better all the time.

He carefully unfolded the twenty, smoothed it out, and laid the bill on the table. As he rose to leave, the waiters saw the gratuity and acknowledged the gift with wide grins. Garrett nodded, but turned away quickly, lest the glare of contempt in his dark eyes be noticed.

"Have fun, boys," he called over his shoulder.

Just before closing the door behind him, he hesitated, listening to the excited talk of the waiters.

"Great guy, that Mike Garrett!"

"They say he's got the delegate job, if he wants it."

"Maybe governor."

"Well, he'd be good either way. He was born and raised in Juneau. The governor ought to be homegrown, instead of some Outside politico."

He strolled toward the Aurora Tavern, taking his time. He walked lightly, catlike, springing ever so easily on the balls of his feet. He seemed to glide rather than hump along, as did other men. He nodded to this couple and that one, enjoying the recognition of the citizens. The walk to the office was bolstering, and he arrived more sure of himself than ever. Today, he was mayor, and he knew just what he wanted out of tomorrow.

Seated at his desk, he cocked his booted feet on its top and let his mind wander.

He had come a long way in just a few years. He was a man of importance in Fairbanks, a big step from his position in Juneau, where he had been nothing. The awful days of his youth would never repeat themselves in his manhood. Here he was rich, and everybody knew it. Back home he had been poor, and everybody knew that, too. They also had known that his father was a drunkard, a misfit, who kept the family in poverty, and got involved in schemes that invariably failed. They knew that his mother kept bread on the table during those years through the kindness of a hundred "uncles." He had known about the uncles, and so did the rest of the town.

He had borne all of that humiliation in silence, but anger found fertile soil in his heart. And that anger flourished until it became the abiding drive in his life.

Garrett was not at all alarmed when he learned that anger ruled. He welcomed the strength it gave him, and when hate paid a visit, he opened the door wide, allowing hate to become an ally.

Anger and hate mingled, forming a coalition so powerful that Garrett rejoiced. He found he could commit acts of viciousness without regret; could hurt without pity; could blaze a trail outside the law with absolute contempt for that same law.

By the time he was twenty, Garrett was a law unto himself. He had no patience with waiting for what he wanted. If certain shortcuts had to be made to bring him the money needed for plans, then those shortcuts would be taken, and they had been. He had early learned something about people that was of tremendous help: boldness quelled disbelief. He knew that not all people thought of him as the great man he'd like them to believe he was. He realized that his credibility was under suspicion because of his association with Sike Hendrickson, but he knew, also, that boldness had undercut suspicions. He openly accepted the man, was seen with him, and the doubters became victims of their own doubt. Surely, a man who gave so handsomely to charity was on the good side of heaven? Possibly, Sike Hendrickson was being condemned unjustly.

Boldness was getting Garrett what he wanted: money. Extortion, bootleg whiskey, crooked card games, whatever, were tools for hastening the time of fulfillment. He wanted to be a real force in Alaska.

Garrett puffed his cigar with relish, and blue clouds drifted in the quiet office air. Yes, he acknowledged, boldness had its uses, but he was no fool and kept his outlaw dealings very quiet. Only those with whom he was involved knew of them, they and Tim Meeker. For a brief moment, irritation dipped the moustache. The fellow was a pain, an honest-to-God pain, with his simpering honesty. But he'd needed Meeker, because his skinny chum had the balance of cash required to open the Aurora. It was a source of deep regret to him that Sike's shot had missed those months back. Had it not been for the Indian girl, Hendrickson would have been on target. Now it would have to be done all over, because not for a minute did he intend Meeker to live. The man was too dangerous. Sike had been willing to try a long rifle shot while Tim was working in the prison street gang. But that would have been too risky. There was a time for everything, and that wasn't it. For that matter, the Indian girl should be punished for interference. Because of her, a simple matter had become complicated. The time would come for her, too.

The door opened, interrupting his inward travels. Ruth entered, and Garrett stood up, stretching tall. He reached for her possessively and was surprised when she backed off, standing away from him.

"Hey, what's this?" he asked.

"Mike, we have to talk." Ruth's lovely eyes were troubled.

"All right, little lady, talk."

"When are we getting married? The whole town finds us the subject of gossip. Did you know that? I've just left a luncheon of the Pioneer Ladies, and I heard whispers in the background." She watched Garrett closely. "That kind of gossip isn't good for you politically, Mike."

Garrett was smooth and gentle.

"Don't let it worry you, my girl. Their empty patter means little. Just as soon as we have a few more dollars . . ."

"Dollars?" Ruth made a face. "Mike, you are one of the richest men in town. What do you want, all of Alaska?"

"Not a bad idea."

Ruth would not be diverted.

"Mike, let's set a date. It is important."

The big man sighed, giving the impression that he could no longer defend himself. He kissed the upturned face and shrugged, saying, "Well, why not! When do you want the wedding?"

"Right away! Just as soon as we can make arrangements."

But Garrett was not to be pushed into it quite so fast.

"How about this fall?" he countered.

"That's such a long time, Mike."

"Only a few months. I tell you what—you make all the arrangements, starting now. That should slow the gossips down."

"Do you mean it?"

"Of course I do. Hire the biggest church, the best musicians, best caterers—everything the best, my dear. We'll have a wedding they'll talk about for ten years. And it will take time to prepare."

"Oh, Mike! You won't regret it. I'll be the perfect wife, you'll see. My hand can do many things."

Caution sharpened Garrett's next words.

"What do you mean?"

"Well, you know. If I can copy Meeker's signature for you, I can do more."

"Ah, yes," said Garrett.

He found a letter on the desk.

"Read this," he said, handing it to Ruth.

She glanced at it and frowned. "It's from that Indian girl, the one who told you about Meeker."

"The same. She'll be back next month and wants a job."

"Are you going to give her one?"

"Perhaps. What do you think?"

Ruth hesitated. "I can't think where it could harm us, though she was on his side once, I gather."

"Yeah, but whatever they had between them certainly died when she turned him in."

Ruth, knowing that Garrett would do as he wished anyway, agreed.

"Good!" exclaimed Garrett. "She can help with the book-keeping and office work."

It was Ruth's turn to be sharp.

"Not all of it!"

"No, not all, not at first, anyway."

Garrett glanced at the wall clock. "I have things to do—and you better get going on those wedding plans."

After Ruth's departure, Garrett thought about two things. He would have to get rid of Ruth. She simply knew too much and she was getting bossy. And hadn't he sensed a threat under that talk about marriage? Yes, there had been a threat.

Item two in the big man's mind concerned Molly Jack. He very much wanted her in his office, and it wasn't only her work that interested him.

When Ruth left Garrett, she went directly to her house. She no longer lived in the cabin that Tim had deeded to her, but a larger residence, not far from her husband-to-be.

Opening a rolltop desk, she withdrew a bound journal from one of the farther cubbies. The book contained records of Garrett's undercover deals. Everything was entered, from extortion money to the cost of bootleg. Though a dangerous kind of book, it was necessary to keep accounts straight. Without it, Garrett would not know who paid him and who he paid from month to month. He knew the book was dangerous, but it was also a protection and vital to his operations.

Ruth smiled and pressed the journal to her breast in a sort of ecstasy. With it in her possession, she had a power that would enable her to get everything she wanted in life, and she wanted all she could get. Had Garrett refused marriage, she'd have set her blackmail schemes into action now. As it was, well, if marriage didn't bring her what she wanted, she still had an ace in the hole.

She returned the book to its hideout, but before closing the desk, she examined another of the same type. This was Garrett's copy, Ruth kept it up to date for him, and he had no idea the second copy existed. He sometimes pored over the transactions for long moments, and when he was finished, he seemed refreshed and energetic, as if a spiritual lack had received fresh sustenance.

It had occurred to Ruth long ago that Mike Garrett was happier as a crook than as an honest man. In her experience, she had found that crooks were usually stupid, and that knowledge was the underlying reason for her switch from Meeker.

CHAPTER 13

When Tim awoke the day after his release from prison, he had a terrible hangover. Thunder roared in the empty spaces of his mind, his mouth was sticky with muck.

A cup of coffee helped, but he was still depressed.

"I feel like I'm in a bog," he told Jake. "My mind is sludge. The thoughts get hung up and go nowhere."

Jake, not feeling all that bright himself, nodded at a quart of whiskey.

"Want a touch of the hair of the dog?"

Tim shuddered negatively and stared at his cup.

Jake had been his main contact with the outside during his jail term. But even *his* visits had been limited. Jake spent most of the winter at Birch Creek trapping, so there were months when he was away. But absence hadn't altered his loyalty, and Tim was aware of that. You didn't find many friends like Jake Lindstrum.

The mandatory confinement of nearly eight months had left Tim almost without a will of his own. He likened himself to a river that split against a series of islands—he wasn't sure where his main channel was. He didn't know his own mind, beyond a capacity for bitterness that surprised him. He was confused, because he'd always thought of himself as a happy person. Cynics were weak people, and the bitter were lost. Was he lost then?

Most of his memories of the past eight months were of bull sessions, work parties, and boredom. But overriding these was the *feel* of that killer's execution. He would never forget the sensation of the courthouse jail shaking to a man's frantic death rhythm. The reverberations of that experience went deep. At night he would wake in a sweat, ready to swear that his bunk was jiggling.

It had been horrifying.

Tim, in an effort to regain a healthy mind, put himself into action. He went to all the banks in town, applying for a business loan. Though he had half expected the response, he was angered when all of them turned him down, tight money being the excuse.

"Doesn't a man's reputation count for anything?" he stormed to Jake. "I've never welched on a loan or any kind of a debt, not ever!"

Mike Garrett and Ruth both had the opportunity to ignore him several times. Ruth's snubbing didn't bother him. In fact, he found her amusing, though Ruth was no joke. Nobody as sly as she could be taken lightly. Her present role struck him as a caricature of prissy righteousness, with an underlay of the devil. He didn't dislike her. She had become a zero, though a dangerous zero—like a cannonball.

One day he met his amiable cellmate, Mickey Jenderson. They invited each other to the Eagle for a drink.

Mickey's beard had matured into a luxuriant growth.

"Looks better on you," Tim said, "than mine did on me."

"Some can wear 'em, some can't," was the reply. Mickey grinned. "You get over the blues yet?"

"Some."

"Like I told you, forget it."

"Nothing bothers you, does it?"

"Oh, I have my limits. Take that drink you just bought me. It is my last today, and that bothers me."

"Are you on the wagon?"

"Going to try—I think."

"You could do well," said Tim, "if you laid off the stuff."

Mickey shook his head, but his eyes were hopeful, giving the lie to the negative.

When Garrett stepped up behind Tim, Tim sensed, rather than saw, his ex-partner. He turned to find the bowie-knife moustache inches away.

"Garrett!" exclaimed Tim, with a thrill of apprehension.

"Yes, Meeky, it's me." The moustache turned down. "When are you getting out of here?"

"Just having a drink."

"I don't mean the Eagle, fella. I mean town. It makes me nervous with a jailbird loose."

Tim stared, unable to move or speak. His cheeks flushed to a shiny red.

"As mayor," Garrett rumbled, "I don't like bums dirtying up the streets. Get out of town."

Garrett's eyes were as hard and bright as drill points.

"And if I don't?" asked Tim huskily.

"I've always been sorry my friend missed you in the office, Meeky. He won't next time."

"Then whoever your friend is, he'll have to get me, too," Jenderson suddenly interrupted.

Garrett ignored him.

Mickey reached over and tapped the big man's shoulder.

"I'm a jailbird, too," he said quietly. "You go for Mr. Meeker, here, and you'll have to do the same with me."

"Who in hell are you?" demanded Garrett roughly. "Keep your damned hands to yourself."

Mickey left his seat and slipped in between Garrett and Tim. His voice was as brittle as a frozen crowbar.

"Since you asked who I am, I'll tell you. I'm a friend of this man, and I'll knock you on your back if you continue badgering him. Your 'friend' can do his worst."

Garrett stared a moment, then growled at Tim, "Do as I say, or you and your buddy here will regret it." He turned on his heel and left the Eagle, full stride.

"Miserable lout!" declared Jenderson. "Can't come in here and threaten my friends."

"He'll get you for that," said Tim.

Mickey snorted. "No, he won't bother me. I'm small fry. But he does want you."

"I'm sorry you're mixed up in this. I can take care of myself."

"I know!" came the explosive response. "But you just weren't in the mood for his foolishness, and I was."

Tim finished his drink. "Listen, I have to go."

"Sure, Tim. Don't let that crook bully you. You're the better man."

"No," Tim heard himself say, "I'm a coward, Mick."

He returned to Jake's heartsick over the incident. Why hadn't he stood up for himself? What had happened to the courage he'd had in the office fight? He hadn't feared Garrett then, nor Sike either. What did it take for him to stand his ground? What kind of a man was he, for God's sake! On and off, off and on, leaving him nowhere.

Jake returned to find Tim packing.

"I'm leaving for Birch Creek" was the explanation. "I need to think things out."

Tim still owned Buck, thanks to Jake, who paid the bill at the Pioneer Stables. Jake had taken the sorrel out occasionally, but only enough to give him exercise and to remind the horse of his manners.

It felt good to be in the saddle again, and Tim sensed that his animal was glad to see him. They'd traveled a lot of miles together. He gave Buck his head and they moved fast, but not fast enough for him to escape two questions: was he leaving because of Garrett's threat? Or was he leaving for the reason he'd given Jake, to think things out? To his shame, he admitted it was probably seventy-five percent the first, twenty-five the second. His spirit tumbled again to such a low that he wondered if he'd ever lose the black mood engulfing him. Probably not. He'd live his life in hell, a confirmed coward and weakling.

But Tim hadn't reckoned on the healing qualities of nature. No better nurse than a leisurely three days in the open, no better prescription than sleeping under the domed sky. Fairbanks and its unhappiness seemed like a bad dream when he arrived at Riley's roadhouse in Central. Disturbing thoughts there still were, just under the surface of consciousness. They slipped into play at unexpected moments, but there was a difference. In town, he hadn't been able to get away from them because there were too many reminders. Now he could shove them out of sight, at least for a time.

Riley was glad to see him, all apologies for his severity the previous fall.

"Hell, Tim, I hope it wasn't my talk that drove you into town and to jail."

"Nope. It was Dwyer."

"Ah, that one!" Riley grimaced. "I found him like you asked, and he was madder than a bull moose in rut. Why, he actually cursed me. The ungrateful fellow didn't even thank me for my kind deed."

"How unbecoming," said a grinning Tim.

He stayed the night talking to the old-timer, enjoying the man's salty views on just about everything. The next day he pointed Buck toward Jake's place.

In parting, Riley said, "Well, at least they can't bother you any more. You paid your debt to society."

"Overpaid," was the acid response. "Society owes me, Riley."

"You going to collect?"

Tim shrugged. The way he felt, he might turn his back on society forever. And who would care?

Jake's cabin, small and squat though it was, seemed like home. Tim even experienced a brief nostalgia, as the unpeeled logs rose out of the wilderness to greet him.

It was good to be back, he thought, even though it was here he'd met his Waterloo under Dwyer's .30-30. The picture of the deputy, mosquito-chewed and red-faced, haranguing Riley, brought another smile. He wondered where Dwyer was now. Probably still beating his chest over the escaped four thousand dollars. Molly Jack put it to far better use, anyway. He thought about Molly and wondered about her, too, and how she was doing.

He soon lost himself in the therapy of work, building Jake more shelves with a few pieces of lumber carried from Riley's. He reinforced the high cache, replacing a rotted stilt with a new one. And he patched the cabin roof, which leaked. The roof was made of poles laid closely together. On top of them lay a foot of dirt. After adding more earth to stop the leaks, Tim followed the custom of many a wilderness man and planted a crop of potatoes in the soil. Riley furnished the seed.

In leisure hours, which were any he chose, he read or went on long hikes. Hiking had been a favorite exercise since boyhood, when he scaled the rocky precipices around Juneau. Walking helped to sort out his thoughts. The good ones were kept at the forefront, ready to overcome the bad. The device didn't always work, but he felt better after a hike, more settled and calm.

By the end of the first week he knew he wasn't alone. He saw the big wolf and his mate, the ones who had been around the year before. The animals appeared at the edge of the forest, apparently curious. But when Tim paused for a better look, they faded into the trees.

There were tracks everywhere Tim went, suggesting a family of wolves, invisible but very much present.

If he didn't see them, they gave voice to howls in the evenings that sent tremors up his spine. The baritone of Blacktail, mingling with the melody of his mate, Yellowchest, sent forth into the world a wild song that went to Tim's heart. God, how free they were! Sometimes, the squeaky yodels of pups joined in, and Tim enjoyed their efforts. Maybe the young ones weren't accomplished in the art of howling yet, but give them A for effort.

There were different howls. Some seemed like triumphant victory declarations, more yappy than musical, and probably signified a successful hunt. Others were directional, Tim thought, as if they were messages to other packs, warning of territorial limits: Keep out! Then some of the choraling seemed to be just for the hell of it, as if the wolves wanted a good howl. They let loose with vigor, drenching the woodlands in a harmonious welter of melody.

There were times when Blacktail soloed. Usually it was late at night, and they were always the same long-drawn notes, hefty and strong. His solo was never interrupted by the others, nor were there other sounds. Even the wind, always a constant on Birch Creek, brushed through the sky on muted wings. Nothing moved in the great silence. It was as if the whole world harked to Blacktail's soliloquy.

Tim was so moved by the beauty of it that at the conclusion of each performance he was tense with emotion. There was in that lone song a yearning for only God knew what.

At these times Tim felt very close to the big wolf and his family, sharing with them the same heaven and earth and the mystery of what was known as life. He didn't try to analyze his kinship, but he did know that it was important to him.

Around the first of July, Jake Lindstrum paid a visit. It was a joyful reunion because Tim was in the midst of a phase that Riley had called the "lonelies." Jake was much impressed by the improvement in his friend.

"You like this life, Tim?"

"You can see for yourself."

"I always thought of you as a city boy."

"I'd like to have both. I like society—I'm not a natural loner. I'd like to have a business again, and this, too. Do you think that's possible?"

"Nothing's impossible." Jake looked at Tim. "That native girl is back in town."

"Molly Jack?"

"Yep. Know what she's doing?"

"I hope she has a good job."

"She's keeping books for our buddy."

"Garrett? Damn it, no!"

"Saw her in the Aurora office myself. She's got one of those typewriters and a desk to sit it on. She looks very efficient."

"So Mike's got her too, eh?" Tim felt the old bitterness welling up. "That son of a bitch gets it all. Why'd she choose him?"

Jake raised his hand.

"Maybe it wasn't so easy for her to find a job. Brown isn't the most popular color with a lot of people. You know that. She can take care of herself, Tim. She's a big girl."

"She's not so big, Jake. She just thinks she is."

His friend threw him a glance. "Oh, it's like that? You're in her corner, aren't you?"

"I made a horse's neck out of myself once, and I'm not proud of it."

"Well, she seems to like the winning team" was Jake's dry response.

"Yeah, well . . ."

The talk moved to other matters, as Tim saw no point in its present drift. But he found himself besieged by an unwanted emotion, and when he discovered it was jealousy, he was not surprised. The thought of Molly in such close contact with Garrett was distracting. A kitten in a bear's den. As he remembered it, Garrett had not avoided the Indian girls of Juneau and had once described them as "pretty good."

He took a couple of belts out of the bottle Jake had brought. They helped numb his mind to the pictures it was showing. Terrible.

In the shank of the evening, the wolves performed nearby.

As the first notes reached Jake, he dashed outdoors with his rifle. He listened intently for a moment, to pinpoint the chorus. Satisfied that he had it, he dashed downriver.

Tim remained at the cabin listening. His mood had taken another dive when Jake seized his gun.

Minutes passed, then the silence was rocked by a shot. This was quickly followed by another. Tim's ears ached, waiting for a third, but it never came and he breathed easier. Jake must have missed and the pack escaped. He put on coffee, because it would help if his friend was disappointed. Coffee and a few jiggers of bourbon worked magic.

There was a soft thudding outside, and he went to the door for a look. There stood Jake, wearing a huge smile. Yellowchest and three pups lay in a heap.

"I got her with one shot," exclaimed Jake happily, "and I clubbed the others when they tried to reach her. Poor dumb things didn't know she was dead." The trapper shook his head. "But that big male got away with a couple of the young ones." He threw back his head and shouted to the forest, "I'll get you yet. Sooner or later, I'm going to turn you into fur."

Tim, meanwhile, stood like a statue, stunned by what he was witnessing.

"That black-tailed one," Jake continued relentlessly, "he's cost me a thousand dollars in fur. I got a shot at him, but I must have missed. Someday I'm going to nail him, and you can bet on it."

"Seems to me you've done pretty well already," observed Tim faintly.

For the rest of the evening, Tim tried to rejoice in Jake's luck, but he was heartsick over the slaughter. More than he'd realized, he'd come to identify with the wolves. He thought of them as companions, who, if not forthrightly friendly, tolerated him and were not afraid of his presence.

Jake skinned the animals and stretched the fur on drying

boards. He gave Tim instructions on what to do with the fur, once it was properly cured.

"And I'll split the money with you," he decided. "If it wasn't for you, I wouldn't have been here at this time of the year. I'd have missed them."

That wasn't lost on Tim, either, and his spirits dropped to zero—so low, that Jake noticed.

"Hey," he said, misunderstanding, "that girl will be all right. Don't worry."

"Oh, it's not her," Tim replied glumly. "Just off my feed, I guess."

Knowing it was his friend's right to remove animals bothering his traps, Tim changed to a subject that would take his mind away from the wolves.

"Are they married yet?"

Jake stared, then curled his lip derisively.

"You mean your former lady and the philanthropist? No, not yet. Seems like I heard talk about a September wedding, big affair. They're probably bickering over who gets control of Garrett's crooked empire. Both are so greedy, they'll each want the full say."

They talked until late, and Tim felt his grief softening, as the bottle dropped its level. But after Jake departed in the morning, he found that he hated his friend. The man who had done the most for him in the world was a killer. Damn him! Damn him! Damn him!

Would he ever hear that wild song again?

CHAPTER 14

Tim waited for the sound of wolf chorus the evening following the slaughter. He timed the hours first, then the minutes, but there were no songs.

He slept badly and was up early. His stomach refused anything but coffee, and very little of that. He had made up his mind: there were two things he had to do, both of them equally important.

First, he must find Blacktail, to settle his mind. Jake had shot at him. The animal could be dead or worse, wounded. The thought of Blacktail in pain and bleeding, gut shot maybe or a leg torn half off, was distressing. For the hundredth time since it happened, he cursed Jake Lindstrum.

Expecting the worst, Tim set out. The den was high on a sloping bank on the cabin side of Birch Creek. He had earlier seen the opening. It was about a mile downstream, and tracks told him who lived there.

He walked swiftly, nearing the den in minutes. No sooner had he started a cautious approach, than he realized eyes were on him. Blacktail or some animal was close.

Not knowing what to expect, Tim levered a shell into action and let the rifle's hammer down to the safety of half-cock.

He stepped lightly, balancing carefully, diminishing chances of a jerky movement that might startle an animal into flight. It was a trick used by the Tlingit Indians on the coast. It came in handy when hunting deer in the shadowed rain forests of the region.

He saw Blacktail suddenly. The wolf was partially hidden in

a thicket of alders. There was a stir beyond him, and Tim noted two pups at play. Tragedy might have cut their family down, but the pups didn't seem to understand it. Exuberant, full of life's juices, the young ones rolled past their parent. In a fuzzy, tail-wriggling knot they plopped into the opening that separated Tim from the family.

Blacktail uttered a growl, and the pups sprang wild-eyed to their feet. When they saw Tim, they yipped and fled to their sire. The parent wolf stood his ground, warily.

"Well," said Tim aloud, "what are your plans?"

Blacktail backed away a few feet. Branches lowered until all Tim could see were the eyes and ears. The eyes, yellow in the sunlight, were steady, the ears perked. Tim stared at Blacktail for long moments, neither moving, then he felt prompted to speak, so he asked softly, "Are you going to stay in this area?"

Immediately, he felt like a fool. The kind of communication established between himself and the wolf, if indeed communication it was, would not be of the chitchat variety. It was sensory and would remain sensory, if he chanced to find similar conditions again. That would probably never be.

Whatever Blacktail felt about the matter would forever remain conjecture. The animal's eyes and ears had disappeared, and Tim knew he was alone.

Tim didn't know all that much about wolves that he counted himself an expert. But for most Alaskans, even city Alaskans, wolves had made themselves known through the drama of their existence, their ways of life. He had read the naturalist Ernest Thompson Seton, and when old-timers talked about them, he had listened. Wolves were strange animals: bright, withdrawn, aggressive, playful, cunning; wasters, savers; savage, gentle; and they mated for life.

Above all, wolves were survivors. They had persisted down through the ages against the changes of evolution and the superior intelligence of another animal, man, against whom few species had ever won the long battle.

With Blacktail gone, Tim turned to the second mission for that day. He wanted some ground to homestead. With the approach of winter, he would need a place of his own. He could no longer impose on Jake. In fact, he wasn't sure he could ever accept Jake as a friend again, after what he was beginning to call the "Birch Creek massacre."

Besides, building a cabin would give him something to do.

The area he had in mind lay directly on the bank of Birch Creek. It was about a mile below Jake's place. There were large, open fields in the region. Once they had been muskeg swamps, but time had shifted the flow of the river to their limits and drained them. With the engineering of more time, dark earth filled between the tufted hummocks, forming an expanse of rich, flat farmland. It was bounded by a forest of spruce, cottonwood, and white birch, promising a free bounty of cabin logs and firewood.

Though homesteading laws allowed claimants one hundred and sixty acres, Tim paced off half that. The law also required that one eighth of the acreage be cultivated. Ten acres would be backbreaking enough, let alone twenty. Besides, he could probably claim the other eighty at a later time.

He marked each of the four corners with a stake and a written notice of homestead on which he gave the approximate measurements. He put the notices in flat tobacco tins to keep them weatherproof and nailed the tins to the stakes. Jake, typical of any wilderness man, never threw anything away, and Tim had discovered a box of the empty cans under the bunk.

After the staking, there was nothing left for him to do except record the ground at the federal land office in Fairbanks. And, of course, to build a cabin and plow up ten acres of ground. There was no hurry for this last provision. He had five years in which to prove up his claim.

For the next five days he selected and cut spruce logs for the cabin. At the end of that time his hands were blistered to a hamburger raw. He was soft, and the blisters painful, but he salved his hands lightly with bacon grease and didn't care a damn. For five wonderful, hard-cutting days, he had forgotten Garrett, Ruth, and Jake Lindstrum. A few blisters were a small price to rid himself of painful memories.

He did not, however, allow his change of heart toward Lindstrum to prevent him from borrowing Jake's tools as he needed them—axes, crosscut saw, and level. His friend—ex-friend!—had a complete set of carpenter's tools. Tim made use of them, though his conscience did bother him some. How could a man dislike somebody, but use his belongings? In this case, he admitted ruefully, necessity was the mother of compromise. Without Jake's tools, there would have been delays, while he bought his own. And Tim wanted no delays. The sooner he had his cabin, the better.

The cabin would face Birch Creek, giving a splendid view of the rugged, snow-capped Crazy Mountains, called the "Crazies" by local sourdoughs. In the evening, the slanting sun bathed the mountains and its shale-topped foothills in a misty, purple wash, beautiful to see. The Crazies were deceiving. They looked, from a distance, like fair game. But Tim had heard prospectors speak of them with the greatest respect. To climb the slab-sided burls of granite was a feat nobody took casually.

Tim was pleased. The setting was idyllic, with forest comfortably ringed around him, forming a horseshoe of security. How would Ruth have done in a place like this homestead? Lovely Ruth. She would have appreciated the view with its charming landscapes, but could she endure the isolation? Most city people couldn't, surprised as they were by the loneliness and unable to cope. The one who could take it in stride was Molly Jack. For her, this would be home and Fairbanks isolation. He wondered how she was doing in Garrett's office, then shrugged her out of mind. There was nothing he could do about Molly Jack, the woman he had told Mickey Jenderson would be his wife.

He had never built a cabin, but he understood the technique

in a general way. He'd seen plenty of them, had lived in several. The Finns in Fairbanks dovetailed the log ends so they made a perfect, tight fit. They were certainly weatherproof, but, also, difficult to build. Dovetailing was the realm of master craftsmen. Tim was anything but that.

Most builders used the conventional notching, hewing a U at each end of a log and laying it face down on its lower companion. Some went so far as to cut a U the entire length of the log, a shallow trench. When cupped over the under log, it fit snugly, forming an airtight wall, that needed no chinking. But that, too, was the work of experts.

In the end, Tim compromised. He decided to notch the ends and cinch the green logs in place with ten-inch spikes. The logs would "wander" as they dried, but the spikes, placed in a zigzag pattern, would discourage this tendency. There would be some traveling, but not enough to matter.

The question arose, where to get the spikes? Jake had none, evidently chancing crooked walls.

On a hunch, he tried Riley's and was greeted with a fortune, not only in spikes, but also in a variety of building materials.

"How come you have all this?" inquired Tim, curious. "Way out here, who's going to need it?"

"I got that stuff," explained Riley, "because of a fluke. A few years ago there was a boom around here. Like all of them it died after the gold petered out."

Birch Creek, far more a river than a creek, was flowing its normal summer depth and speed. Tim took advantage of the waterway by building a raft. Using Riley's wagon and horses, he hauled several loads to his craft. When he was ready to shove off, he had doors, window glass, stove and pipe, lumber, nails of all sizes, galvanized roofing. Though he hadn't a penny to his name, Riley gave it all to him on credit.

"Your word is your reference" was all the old-timer said.

Not being a raftsman of any experience, Tim had reason to regret his enormous load. Birch Creek was swift, and it was stitched with sweepers, trees that had toppled across the current. When he saw one looming, Tim stood in the bow, and, like a medieval knight, jousted the tree with his steering pole. Most of the time the tactic worked, and the raft spun around the sweeper harmlessly.

But if the pole slipped and the raft coasted into the tree, the current would immediately pressure the upside. Unable to budge, the raft would tip, water spraying in white, foaming fans. By pulling on the branches of the tree, Tim could shift around the end and slip free before tipping over. He thanked God for taking Riley's advice to build the raft wide and to lash his cargo securely. A wide raft was difficult to capsize.

He reached the homestead after rafting twenty nerve-racking miles. He was weary and soaking wet, but victorious. In one calculated, if dumb, effort, he had his entire outfit in place. There was enough material to complete his cabin, and then some. Tim wasn't an overly religious man, but he had his moments and now was one.

He looked up at the sky and said, "I know I said some mean things on that raft. I apologize, and thank you for looking after a fool."

Tim should have been satisfied, but he wasn't, not quite. Money was becoming a problem. He wanted to pay Riley, because debt simply galled him. He might be penniless, but he did still own half of the Aurora Tavern. Nothing had ever been done to dissolve the partnership. Jailbird or not, he was legally a partner of Garrett's. That wasn't good, either. As a partner, he was still responsible for what Garrett did, the same as if he was there. The time was long overdue for a settlement.

CHAPTER 15

At the end of July, after laying the foundation of the cabin, Tim mounted Buck and traveled to Fairbanks. There was no need to sneak in this time, and he reached the Pioneer Stables by main avenues.

Instead of going to Jake's, he signed for a room at the Nordale Hotel. He still didn't trust himself with his friend. That bothered Tim, but he reckoned the danger was real, that he might throw a punch. So he took the prudent course.

Before taking any action, he bellied up to a restaurant counter and ordered a feast of steak, eggs, potatoes, two pieces of dried peach pie, and several cups of coffee. It was his first decent meal in a long time, not counting visits to Riley's place. Early on, Tim discovered that as a cook, he'd make a good teamster. Even boiled water seemed to come out wrong.

He set upon the steaming platter with enthusiasm and finished with a great sigh of satisfaction. He was ready to battle Siberian tigers. He paid the tab with money borrowed from Riley and headed for the land office.

The man in charge of the land office was an acquaintance of Tim's—Al Stegner, an affable chap, who pored over the plats with love and knowledge.

"Not many homesteads over that way," commented Stegner. "Leach has the Springs, Riley has the Central roadhouse." He looked up. "No hot springs on your ground?"

Tim shook his head, "Wish there were."

"No, you don't. Leach got one of the last allowed by law."

"How come?"

The land man shrugged. "Couldn't say, but all hot springs are dried up as far as homesteading is concerned."

Tim paid his fee for filing, saw that his name was recorded, and left. He felt good. He now had something: land. He felt just a little less like a floater, and he liked that. And now that that was taken care of, there was some business at the Aurora Tavern.

On the way, he met Mickey Jenderson. His former cellmate looked the picture of healthy living.

"I'm working the riverboats stevedoring," he explained with his usual good humor, "that'll get a man in shape right quick!"

"How about the booze?" asked Tim.

"Booze? Oh, well, yes, I have a drink now and then." Mickey stroked his curly red beard. "But you know something? I don't seem to hit it like I did. Maybe I'm getting old."

"Maybe you're learning that life and booze don't mix."

"Am I getting a sermon?"

"Not from me, you're not. Just making an observation born of great wisdom."

"Ha!" Mickey snorted. "Where you heading?" he wanted to know.

Tim revealed his plans, finding no reason for secrecy.

Mickey was doubtful.

"That bastard's got the first nickel he ever stole."

"Who, the great philanthropist?"

"Oh, yeah, well, I'll tell you about that, if you don't know already. He makes sure his giving hits all the newspapers. Nothing wrong with that—if it was anybody else but hairy lip. That damn crook is buying his way to the governorship, Tim."

Meeker agreed that was something that Garrett could and would do.

"When he sees you," remarked Mickey, "he ain't going to love it. Remember the last time?"

Tim would never forget how his friend had shouldered between himself and Garrett.

"And now," concluded Jenderson, "you want lots of money from him."

"I'll take my chances," muttered Tim, but his palms were getting sweaty. He was half sorry that he'd bumped into Mickey now. "I'll see you," he said gruffly, sticking out his hand.

Jenderson grasped it, and for a second his eyes sharpened. "You want me along?" he asked.

"No. I'll handle it, Mick. Thanks."

But the closer to the Aurora he got, the tighter his stomach. He cursed himself, and the chance meeting with his friend. Damn it! To think of Garrett was to dread the man. Would he be there? Sike? Ruth and Molly? He just hoped there'd be no audience, just Mike and he. How would he broach the subject—come right out with it like: "Garrett, you owe me ten thousand dollars for my half of the business"? That black moustache would wrinkle up on that one, dance a jig, probably. Sike Hendrickson's icy eyes would get misty with the thought they'd see blood that day. A real joy, that fellow.

Suddenly, Tim changed course and wound up in John Clark's office.

"You look great!" cried the lawyer. "That outdoor life is making you into a new man."

Tim nodded and thought, *Perhaps in some ways.* He came right to the point.

"I want to sell my half of the tavern."

"Yes, I've wondered about that. Best to get out I think. I see no problems—go to it."

Tim hesitated.

"Do you want something out of me?" questioned the lawyer.

"Well, you can handle the details."

"Starting when?"

"Right now."

Clark swept his hand over the scattered papers on his desk.

"I'm buried so deep, Tim, the worms look down to say howdy. How about next week?"

"No. I want this thing over with, John."

"Well, go ahead. I'll handle the legals, on whatever arrangements you make."

"I want you to go with me."

Clark glanced warily at his desk.

"Go with me," insisted Tim, "or I'll get another attorney."

"Hey," protested Clark, "don't go gritty on me. I'm your friend, even if I do charge for services rendered."

He gathered the papers into a pile and headed for the door.

"Let's go and see Mr. Garrett. I want to have a look at his face, when you spring this on him."

The man in question was in the office. So were Ruth and Molly. Hendrickson was absent.

One down, thought Tim.

The meeting was anything but friendly.

"What you want, Meeky?" growled the big man. "Thought I ordered you out of town long ago."

Tim felt his mouth go dry.

"I'm here on business," he managed.

Ruth and Molly both glanced at him. Ruth flushed and left without a word. Molly nodded at him quickly, but bent over her desk again. Tim noted she was using what Jake had called a "typewriter" quite well. She punched at the keyboard rapid fire.

"You learn that in school?" Tim asked of the curved back.

"I said speak, Timmy!" interrupted Garrett nastily. "Or did you come to ogle the help?"

John Clark, silent until now, spoke up. "Mr. Meeker wants to sell his half of the Aurora."

The big man's eyes widened, and the bowie-knife moustache did a jig, as Tim thought it would.

"Never heard anything so funny!" roared Garrett. He jabbed a thick finger at Tim. "You own nothing here, fella."

"I own half, Mike. I've papers to prove it."

Garrett shook his head emphatically.

"You don't own a thing, *Mister* Meeky."

Tim flushed under the hard eyes.

"It would be a simple matter to show he does," intervened Clark. "Your license bears both names."

"Not this one!" shouted Garrett, pointing to a framed document hanging on the wall in back of his desk.

Tim felt queasy. Had the man somehow bilked him out of his share?

The license, issued for the current year, listed only Michael Garrett as owner and proprietor of the Aurora Tavern.

"That means nothing," retorted Clark. "A license is not a bill of sale. You ought to know that, Garrett. Papers of partnership, on file in the city hall records, will show Mr. Meeker's name. And without a bill of sale to show transfer of property, you haven't a legal right to his interest."

Garrett allowed the moustache to curve up slowly.

"You are mistaken, Clark," he responded smoothly. "I can show you the bill of sale, signed by Meeky himself."

Hearing a sound behind, Tim turned to see the pale eyes of Hendrickson boring into him.

"Show him the paper, Garrett," suggested Sike, "and then get out of here, Meeker. That's a terrible stink you brought in. A stink like that is only caused by the color of yellow."

Garrett spoke to Molly. The girl quickly leafed through a file, found what she wanted, and handed it to Garrett. Then she resumed her furious typing.

Garrett handed the document to Clark, who read it and gave it to Tim, puzzled.

"It looks good," he said. "I don't understand."

Tim snatched the paper, heart racing. He stared in disbelief. There were the words, stating matter-of-factly that he, Timothy Meeker, had sold to Michael Garrett his interest in the tavern for ten thousand dollars. It was dated December 15, the year before, and his signature was laid out on the bottom line in the original.

"This is a forgery," he protested. "I never signed anything. I was in jail then. How could I sign any papers?"

Garrett nodded. "Oh, you were in the clink, all right. Don't you remember me coming over? But, then, you were so shaken up, Meeky, I doubt if you remember anything at all."

"The guard will remember."

"I'm sure he will. We can go over to jail right now and prod his memory—whoever happens to be on. Of course, there was a lot of people in and out of that place, but I'm sure I'll be remembered."

Tim caught on at once. It would be his word against Garrett's. An ex-con against a prominent citizen, and who would be believed?

"Bull!" cried Tim in frustration. "You're lying, Garrett!"

"Get out of here," hissed Hendrickson, "or I'll jam your teeth down your skinny throat."

Garrett spoke to Clark.

"Everything is legal," he said, "so why don't you get my ex-partner out of here."

Clark nodded.

"We better leave it for now," he said to Tim. "We'll check the public records just to make sure, but," his eyes narrowed on Garrett, "I'm sure that all is in order."

Garrett smiled.

"You can bet they are, counselor. You can bet on that."

CHAPTER 16

Using a drawknife, Tim peeled the logs before raising the walls of his cabin. Peeled logs resisted weather better, were more durable. They also looked better, with cleaner lines than unpeeled logs.

Spring sap had long since receded in the logs, and the bark had to be removed piece by piece, a slow, muscle-jarring task. Had he cut his logs in late April or May, the bark would have peeled in easy sap-wet slabs. He grumbled to the world of trees and fields surrounding him, but the world paid no attention. From the first to last log he whittled away every square inch of bark.

The trouble was worth it. The logs, though not as smoothly shaven as they would have been in sap time, displayed a blond-sepia facade, pleasing to the eye. They were better than clean-peeled logs, which, after all, were really too blond. He smiled at the notion: at least, that was what he was going to believe.

The humiliation of defeat by the machinations of Garrett stuck to him like a sickness. Mike had beaten him once again.

The forged bill of sale was a masterpiece of deception. The signature was so perfect that he almost admired the hand that had skillfully signed him out of ten thousand dollars. It was clear to him that Ruth had been the forger. She was an artist, and though not so great an artist as Sydney Laurence, she had superb control. Ruth, his once true love! How she must have smiled when she traced his name.

Tim tried to be fatalistic about events as they had unfolded. What was, was. He tried not to think about his loss or heed his

deep sense of separation. He missed the world from which he'd
been forced. It had been a good life for him. He liked the action of business and the men with whom he dealt. The inter-
course with humanity was important, for he was gregarious by
nature. If not exactly a herd animal, he knew the value of the
herd. It was where things happened.

To help him forget, Tim resorted to the therapy of work
again. Hard work. Sunup to sundown. He went to bed exhausted and slept like the logs he handled every day.

They were no cinch. The green timbers were heavy, two to
three hundred hefty pounds each. The lower part of the walls
was not difficult, but he had a battle placing the last few top
rounds. The logs fought back, refusing to stay in place, toppling
to the ground before he could spike them in place. He wrestled
them one by one, driving the spikes deep, with a vehemence to
match his frustration over Fairbanks events.

At the end of five days, the last log had been laid and secured.
Tim lost two shirts in the process, ripped and mutilated past
any usefulness. He was skinned and bruised from head to shin
as a result of manhandling the timber in a total effort to get the
damned things where he wanted them.

When he looked at the four walls after the battle, though, he
was pleased. The corners were square and true. The logs were
so firmly spiked that they could withstand the convolutions of a
Yakutat earthquake.

In spite of the self-administered therapy, Tim found it was
successful only to a point. No power he mustered blacked out
remembrance completely. Every now and then, when he least
expected it, a door in his mind was swung open by some sar-
donic devil, and there they all were, Garrett, Hendrickson,
Ruth, all smiling sly as foxes.

The cabin was finished in the last week of August. Tim la-
bored twelve hours a day setting the roof, laying in double windows, one in each wall, for good light. The roof was not dirt

like Jake's, but lumber, covered with sheets of corrugated iron. Standing back to admire the place, pride warmed his heart. Not bad for a beginner. The shining roof, the new logs, the glistening windows presented a picture that gave him a feeling he'd never experienced before. The cabin was his creation start to finish. This was his fort and refuge. From here, he could hold off the world.

He built two bunks, one over the other to save space, and was able to get springs and mattresses from Riley. In fact, Riley had everything he needed, from toilet paper to Dutch ovens. One man's defunct gold rush was another man's good luck.

The evening that he drove the last nail, Tim had a whiskey to celebrate. As he relaxed over his glass, Blacktail howled. The wolf's baritone floated from the north, across the river. He was probably on the promontory that served as a sometime lair.

Two more voices joined in, the cracking pitch of the young. Though not exactly Wagnerian, or even Scott Joplin, Tim was, as always, thrilled. The chorus was a grand refrain to him. He listened intently for five or six minutes, then it faded away. There followed a silence, broken only by a belated yap or two from the pups.

Late that night the primitive music once more filled the forests with sound. It was quite close, on Tim's side of the river, downstream.

The nights were now dark, and Tim didn't know what to expect when he opened the door. He lit a lamp and held it aloft, peering at the outer bounds of the yellow light.

It was quiet, only Birch Creek's low-water whisper broke the silence. Even the pervading hum of mosquitoes had been stilled by first frosts.

He was fully aware of his ridiculous appearance: a full-grown man in baggy underwear, holding a kerosene lamp over his head in the wee hours. It didn't matter.

A faint rustle to his left, away from the river, caught his ear.

After a moment's delay he was rewarded by the glow of eyes reflecting light.

At first, there was just one pair, spookily disembodied. They seemed to float across the darkness, two blue-green orbs turned, always, toward him.

In a few seconds, these were trailed by two additional sets. Six circles of intense fire drifted past. Then they abruptly winked out, as the owners disappeared into the forest.

Tim returned to his sleeping bag, delighted. He liked their presence, though he did admit to a slight uneasiness at times. Wolves were, after all, untamed and unpredictable. If Blacktail had paid a night visit, it was to assess the danger, not the friendship. There would probably never be trouble, but neither would the wolves become pets. Blacktail was no man's dog. Even so, Tim felt less alone, because of them.

After the main cabin had been completed, he built, in succession, a barn for Buck, a high cache, and an outhouse. He put a stove in the barn so that the sorrel would be comfortable. Though the horse's body heat was enough to warm the small structure in zero temperatures, sixty below wasn't to be fooled with.

When all the buildings were finished, Tim went hunting. Within a mile of the homestead, he downed a moose, a nice fat three-year-old. He soon had him hanging from poles under the cache. That night, he enjoyed fresh sirloin steak, a welcome change from canned corned beef and ham. Delicious! As far as he was concerned, even the best beef took second place.

Next, he went after caribou. Though not so nutritious as moose, caribou would make a fine supplement. As much as one liked moose, he couldn't eat it three hundred and sixty-five days of the year. And, besides, if the meat wasn't as nourishing as moose, nature offered no finer dish than baked caribou heart.

The large Forty Mile caribou herds, totaling a hundred thousand strong, were in full migration. They bore east, toward winter ranges in Canada and the steep-hilled country from which the herd took its name.

Though migratory trails were not lined up with the homestead, Tim hadn't journeyed for more than an hour on foot before he drew a bead on a large, ring-necked bull. He was about to shoot another, when he lowered the .45-70. One moose, one caribou, that was plenty.

At the conclusion of two days' hunting, Tim hung the rifle up. He had wanted a mountain sheep, but the Crazies were mantled in snow. Even if he rode Buck into the high country, chances of reaching sheep ranges weren't good. As surefooted as they were, the sheep would scale the very summits of the mountains to escape. He would try for one next year.

And now it was garden time.

Though there had been several heavy frosts, Jake's roof-top potato crop lost only its top foliage. He was able to fill three gunnysacks with potatoes. The roof crops were a bonus, found money, because he had neither watered nor weeded the garden all summer. It grew on its own.

With his winter meat cooling, three hundred pounds of spuds under the bunk, and credit for a winter's supply of grub at Riley's, Tim's confidence strengthened. From being completely wiped out, he had started a new life. It was a life he had shaped with his own two hands, and it was a great feeling.

CHAPTER 17

The day after the roof crop was harvested, Jake Lindstrum arrived and blew a hole in Tim's cozy sense of well-being. The trapper's eyes were hostile, the warmth of friendship very cool.

"I hear you was in town," he said accusingly.

Tim immediately sensed trouble and reacted warily.

"That's right."

"Why didn't you let me know?"

Some of Tim's anger had faded during the long, active period since Jake had killed the wolves. He no longer wanted to punch him, and he parried his friend's barbed thrust with "Just didn't think I should bother you."

"Bother me!" Jake gave a hard, unpleasant laugh. "Why you ignorant son! Here I stuck my neck in the noose for you and you ignore me. That's a rotten way to treat a man.

"And what's this?" continued Jake, waving a blunt-fingered hand. "How come you built this place?"

"I'm homesteading," replied Tim, feeling his neck growing hot. What the hell?

"Homesteading!" Lindstrum's ruddy face had taken on the bright flush of a man catching fire inside. "You're on my property. My trap line begins downriver only a few hundred yards from here."

"That doesn't put me on your property then, does it! I checked at the land office, Jake, and I'm in the clear."

Trap lines didn't show on land plats, but Tim didn't know what else to say. There was battle in the air, and he knew it and didn't want it, either.

Jake was facing the south window, the one looking up the back trail toward his own place. Suddenly he stared, then swore. He grabbed Tim's rifle and leaped outdoors, all in one motion. Tim knew instantly what was happening and ran after Jake just as he was aiming. Blacktail was poised motionless fifty yards away, eyes slitted, bushy tail angling down.

"Jake!" cried Tim. "Don't!"

As he shouted, he knocked the rifle aside. The heavy-calibered gun roared, but the bullet raced harmlessly into the sky. Blacktail disappeared, unharmed.

Jake glared first at the spot where the wolf had been, then at Tim. Furious, he let out a yell and dove.

Tim toppled under the force. Even as the hard earth struck from beneath, he thought, What in the world am I doing fighting Jake?

But fight he did. He had to, because his chief benefactor would have it no other way.

The two rolled on the ground, pounding each other with knotted fists. Tim had gained weight during the summer, in spite of poor cooking. His muscles had strengthened in response to hard work. Though Jake was the hardier of the two, Tim was as tall, and his reach about the same.

The fight was nearly equal, with one difference. Lindstrum had done this before, and experience was definitely in his favor. He struck where the blows had the best effect—the stomach, the upper arms, the face, all calculated to wear his hard-breathing adversary down. Tiring the opponent when the fight was equal gave one a decided edge.

Tim felt his knees buckling, though he felt little pain. He kept his fists working, but without any sure knowledge of where to strike he punched indiscriminately, without serious effect. He was weakening.

Then came a particular blow, one that professional boxers like to give but not receive. It was a right hook to the jaw, a blow that carried two hundred pounds of tough man muscle and a weight of anger that couldn't be measured. It landed directly on the point of Tim's chin, and lit with such a crack, the quiet forest echoed. Tim slumped, the fight over for him.

When he came back to the light of reason, he was lying on his bunk, staring at the ceiling.

"Be damned," he muttered thickly, "I seem to be doing this sort of thing more than average the past year or two."

"You all right?" Jake's bruised face was anxious. "You been out for a while. Had me scared."

"You afraid of anything?" mumbled Tim through swollen lips.

"Sure."

"Don't make me laugh." Tim winced. He was certain his lips had been stuffed with ground glass. "I'm the guy who's timid. Remember me, Timid Meeky?"

"Yeah, well, listen . . ." Jake rubbed his jaw gently. "I'm pretty well clobbered, see?" He turned his face this way and that, revealing cuts and bruises. "That wasn't done by a scared man. You were mad, and I want to know why."

Tim sat up and considered the weaving floor before replying. Jake offered whiskey, which he took. The alcohol warmed his system, and diluted some of the fuzziness in his mind.

Finally, he said, "You're right, I was mad."

"But why in hell?" wondered Jake.

"I'll put it to you straight: I was, and still am, mad as hell at you for killing those wolves last summer."

Jake glowered. He got up and stirred the fire, throwing some wood on. The fire crackled hungrily, throwing heat back in turn for its meal.

"Why, Tim," said Lindstrum at length, "that's my business, man. It's what I do. I'm a trapper, and sometimes I have to do what you seen. It isn't pretty work."

Tim checked out his feelings on the course their dialogue was taking. He was calm and clearheaded now. What he was saying seemed necessary, and the fight with Jake had been necessary, too. Otherwise, Blacktail would now be dead. He was ashamed of his anger, but not the fight. Being beaten didn't seem important.

"I know about your work," he said. "I trapped too when we were kids, and I know lots of trappers. But, damn it, Jake, those wolves were my company out here." He held up his hand when Jake snorted. "I know it sounds crazy, but that's the way it was and is. When you dumped half that pack on the ground dead, hell, everything turned upside down for me. I hated you. I'd figured you to be the kindest man in the world, and then you did that."

All Jake said was, "Yeah, well . . ."

The two friends left off talking. Jake fixed drinks for both, and they slipped into a mutual silence, listening to the fire gobble the green spruce.

The cabin warmed. Evening approached and the country was quiet in the twilight. The raspy talk of mallards on the river cranked through the gloaming. A squirrel chattered, and Tim remembered he was going to wrap tin around the cache's corner posts. Squirrels couldn't climb over tin. Their claws couldn't dig in. You had to keep them out or they messed things up.

Blacktail howled with his children and another voice joined them. It was different, almost like the voices of the pups, but it didn't crack. Had the big wolf taken another mate?

"That's what you like?" asked Jake, breaking the silence.

"I like that, yes, and I don't want you killing the black-tailed one. I'll fight you again if I have to. Don't shoot him."

For an instant, Jake's face hardened, then the tough features relaxed.

"Well, I'll be damned," he said.

"Why?"

"I think you are growing up, Timmy."

"Meaning?"

"Do you realize that thieving rascal is the first thing you've ever stood up for?"

Tim shook his head. "Hadn't thought about it." He squinted at his cup. "But maybe you are right." Then he added quickly, "I mean what I say about him."

Jake shrugged. "Don't worry about it. I don't think he's the point any more."

"Then what is?"

"God, you can be dense! I'm talking about Garrett."

Tim flushed. "Oh, no you don't. I've had it with that fellow. Past is past, and that's it."

"You mean you don't need him any more?"

"*Need* him! What are you talking about?"

Jake poured more whiskey. When the cups had been replenished to his satisfaction, he said, "You are a user."

"What's a 'user'?"

"You are. Do you realize that you've been using Garrett?"

"That's bunk!"

"Bunk or not, think about it. You knew Garrett went bad way long ago, Tim, a year before your blowup. Right?"

Tim admitted it.

"But you didn't do anything about it," continued Jake, "because you were using Garrett's know-how. He was bringing you good money, more than you've ever had, and you liked that. He was tough, and you liked that, too. A tough front man, somebody aggressive to act and take hold. You were hiding behind him. You were using him, my friend."

"That is simply not true!" objected Tim. His voice rose.

"And there's more!" Jake insisted. "You used me, too. You came to me for help . . ."

"You carried me out of the Aurora. I didn't ask you to do it."

"That's true, but you've been damned glad to take what I could offer since. I let you use my cabin at no little risk, and what do I get for it? You blow up when I clear some pests that were bothering my traps. Don't you realize that it's a waste of life when wolves, or anything else, ruin the fur? It has to be stopped."

Tim sat dumb, the accusations washing over him like some sort of a paralyzing virus. Jake rushed on. It was as if he'd been storing up and couldn't hold the flood.

"I've been a front man for you, too. Not that I minded, you know that, but you still aren't standing on your own feet."

Jake's anger-bright eyes swept the cabin.

"You got a nice place here, a neat little nest, where you can hide out for the rest of your life, and to hell with Garrett and those nasty people who messed you all up. You'll show them, by God. You'll just turn your back on them."

When Tim started to protest, Jake cut him short.

"And you used Riley, too," the trapper continued relentlessly. "Oh, yes! Riley was another front, Tim. You went running to him first thing. It didn't matter that you got him in dutch with the law."

"The hell it didn't," flashed Tim, coming out of his paralysis. "I didn't want Riley involved, and I fixed it with Dwyer about that."

"I'll grant you that much, but you did use him and me. Not that we minded, we were glad to help, but God damn it, Tim, we also expected you to fight back, and you didn't."

Tim said nothing, both fascinated and repelled by his friend's tirade.

"And I'll tell you more," Jake said, "as long as I'm unloading: you used Ruth, too."

"*Ruth!*"

"Sure. Consider. She is a beautiful woman. You've never been a whiz with the ladies, but when Ruth came into your life, your ego swelled like a pregnant moose's belly. With her, you gave out the impression that you were quite a man, and you liked that. I don't think you ever really loved her—you loved the idea of her is all." Jake drew back on that when he saw the forces of protest in Tim's eyes. "All right, maybe you did love

her. I can't say about that, can I, though you have to admit,
Tim, love is a mature quality, and I don't think you are mature.
Anyway, regardless, you used her, pure and simple. You been a
user all your life."

"Not all my life."

"Well, I can't say about that either, but do you see what I'm
driving at?"

Tim remained silent. It was coming pretty fast.

At length he said, "You're hitting pretty hard."

"And I've got more. Garrett intimidates you. He always has,
since we were kids. He's always been the 'big man' to you.
Right?"

Tim nodded. He had always admired Mike.

"And so what is happening?" said Jake in a softer voice, his
indignation and anger diminishing the more he talked them out.
"You're knuckling under to him, because it is a habit."

"Habit?"

"Sure. You're supposed to be panicked by Garrett. That's
the game you and he play. He's the boss, and you the admiring
dummy. That was all right when you were kids, but you're a
man now, Tim. You have to act for yourself."

The two again followed the more agreeable ministrations of
silence. Tim let himself go along with it, thinking. He recalled
the time he'd punched Garrett, when Garrett was with Ruth.
He hadn't been afraid then. He was so mad, he'd forgotten the
game Jake said they played. And just before he went to jail,
there'd been no fear in the office fight. For a time his emotions
had taken a neutral corner. But when he'd gone to see about
selling his interest in the Aurora, there had been too much time
to think himself into a panic. Like Jake said, he toadied to
Mike's authority.

Tim's face glowed with a blush of pure embarrassment. To
think he'd played the clown! How many knew that, while he
didn't?

Jake broke into his analysis.

"What's going on in your thick skull? You look like you just ate a mink tail."

"Yeah . . . Maybe you're right."

"About the mink tail?"

"No, damn it, about Garrett."

"You bet your stinking socks I am."

"So where does that leave me?"

"You ought to have a showdown with him. Don't you still own half the Aurora?"

"No."

Tim told Jake about the forgery.

Jake swore long and successfully, and when he was through, even Tim felt better.

"Listen," Jake pointed a finger at him, "I'm not the one you should be fighting but our old chum Garrett. The sooner the better."

Tim looked away, saying faintly, "What would I gain?" As much as he knew his friend was right, the thought of facing his former partner dismayed him.

"Tim, you've got to do it!"

"I tried that, and look what happened to me."

"You had the cards stacked against you then. It isn't that way now. Listen, you have the key, yourself. Find Mike's records of his underhanded deals, and you can lock him up."

Tim said nothing.

Jake glanced around the cabin approvingly. "You have a nice place here, and it took a man to build it. There's nothing easy about putting up a cabin. I know, because I've done it."

He slapped his knee in exasperation.

"What does it take to get you off your butt!" He knotted his skinned knuckles. "This is a great place and you've got a right to be proud of it, but you can't hide here, Tim. I know you well enough to say this: if you hide here, you'll be bothered by what-could-have-beens for the rest of your life. You're a better man than you know."

Jake stopped, and his voice calmed.

"All right, I've yelled all I'm going to yell. It's up to you, now."

"Don't shoot the wolf" was all Tim said.

CHAPTER 18

Mike Garrett was confident that the world was his apple. As he sat in the Aurora Tavern's office, contemplating the tight curve of Molly Jack's spine, he knew that, sooner or later, he would be governor of Alaska. Possibly congressional delegate. The moustache curled. Why not both?

There were problems, however. The most immediate was Ruth. She had grown possessive, and he didn't like being possessed. She was dangerous to his future because she knew too much. There had been a time when he thought she could still be useful. He had been willing to take a chance, but ever since her laughable insistence on marriage, he distrusted the supposed light of his life. Did she think he couldn't see through her ploys? He was perfectly aware that Ruth was capable of blackmailing him. After all, the mentality that could forge a bill of sale for ten thousand dollars was a mentality to be watched. Nor would marriage deter her. If things didn't go her way, she'd still be a threat. Hell, give the woman time, and she would be running the operation, not him.

Garrett's eyes caressed Molly's back. He had never intended marrying Ruth. The September proposal was a delaying tactic. It was working, and he'd had time to think matters through. It was sad, but Ruth had to go—all the way. Sike would take care of that. The man was a natural killer, and he wanted the job.

After Ruth, there was Meeky. Timid was not a fool. A bit weak, perhaps, but no fool. Chances were, he'd try to expose the forged bill of sale. He and Ruth had been close once, and there was certainly a possibility, at least, of a collaboration between the two. Even with Ruth at the bottom of the Chena, Timid continued to be a threat. He'd pick away until he somehow exposed that damned piece of paper.

Garrett's eyebrows beetled.

There was more. Meeker and Lindstrum were two of a kind. When they had been kids they'd called themselves the three musketeers. What rot! He had never considered himself a real part of the trio. He never considered himself a part of anything. He was a separate boy, just as he was a separate man. As a boy, he had to pretend to be a member of the crowd, because it got him what he wanted, a juvenile power that put him at the top. He'd been a leader in everything. But it was Timmy and Lindstrum who pushed the most for him. Their influence had made him a success. Damn them!

Timid! Garrett made a clucking noise with his tongue. He'd used him for all he was worth. Meeky would do anything he asked, go along with any scheme. But when he'd chosen the skinny punk to become his partner, it was only after a long deliberation. He'd turned his back on school chums when he left school. They never got another thought until this Fairbanks rush came up. Then he'd needed capital, and Meeky had it (God knows where he got that kind of money). Using his new partner's money, along with what he had, made possible the foundation of his (still) small empire. He owned the tavern, several offices in the downtown area, and several houses. All were income producing. And, while thinking about income, one shouldn't forget the, ah, other arrangements. Money was rolling in, and he was just getting started.

As it was turning out, though, Meeky could upset the whole apple cart. His ex-buddy was a danger, so he, too, would have to go. Possibly, he should have had the punk killed right after he got out of jail. There were plenty of opportunities, but caution held him back. It would have looked bad for him if Meeky had disappeared or, worse, been found with a bullet hole in his head so soon after leaving prison. The time hadn't been right, and for something like murder you had to have everything in your favor.

Meeky was in Central, living with Riley, he'd heard. Fine. Garrett had friends in Circle who would be glad to help out. It was what friends were for. No need to worry.

So it followed that if Meeky was removed, Lindstrum would have to go, too. That ape-handed trapper would get suspicious. Well, good old Sike knew how to handle snoopy people, and that brought the matter to a full circle: Sike, himself, would be the last to go. He was a good man for certain things, but he was no good at all for an aspiring politician. Hendrickson would be the last, and he, Michael Garrett, would tend to it personally.

Garrett's bowie-knife moustache took a dive. God damn Meeky and Lindstrum! All through their boyhoods they'd had it good, while he, easily the most talented and presentable, ate humble pie. His daddy and mama were from the "other side of the tracks" while his buddies had happy homes. But he had been nobly accepted by Meeky and Lindstrum into their lovely little circle. Hot damn!

Garrett growled at the unpleasant memories his mind was dredging up. Molly turned around to see what prompted the sound.

Her employer's eyes were black as coal. His ruddy face was undergoing a slow change to an untoward crimson flush.

"Why do you look at me like that, Molly?" he asked huskily.

"I hear you make sound. I think maybe you are sick."

"Oh, I'm sick all right." Garrett emitted a sound very much like a giggle. "But my sickness can be cured easily, with the right kind of help." When Molly made no reply, he said, irrelevantly, "I have enemies."

"Oh, I don't know," said the girl encouragingly. "Who not like you? You give much money to good causes."

"I never gave any to Meeky, when he asked for it."

"You don't owe him that."

"But he thinks I do. You heard him. He wanted me to pay him for this place the second time."

Molly's face showed she doubted some aspects of that remark, but she said nothing.

Garrett was quick to pick it up.

"You don't believe I paid him, is that it?" His voice rasped like a file on wood.

"I don't say that."

"But you like him."

"I don't say that," Molly repeated.

She gazed at the big man a moment, then asked quietly, "When you give me the rest of the four thousand, Mr. Garrett?"

"Like I told you!" The voice was sharp. "When you decide to be nice to me."

"I not do that."

The moustache came close to a leer.

"What do you mean you 'not do that,'" mimicked the mayor of Fairbanks. "I never knew a squaw who wouldn't, especially when two thousand dollars was the reward."

"You don't know me."

Garrett smirked and rose. He paced the floor nervously, his shiny boots thumping hard.

"You lie to me," he said. "You know you do, but you're being stubborn. You want more money?"

Molly reddened and, not knowing what to do next, returned to her work, replying faintly, "Only what's mine."

At that juncture, Sike Hendrickson entered. His malevolent dog eyes swept the room, missing nothing. It was said, among knowing circles in town, that Sike's eyes were a sure mirror to the man. He was cruel and enjoyed inflicting pain. It was no secret that he once beat a horse to death with a club. The animal had stumbled, and Sike, drunk, had fallen to the ground. The horse's screams could be heard for a long time.

It was also rumored that he had been in trouble Outside. He

had killed a man in a Montana holdup. He was also suspected of arson in several western towns. All of the fires involved were hotels, and in each lives had been lost.

All rumors, however, were left as rumors, because the man the law was looking for was named John Sikes, and there wasn't enough description to make positive identification. Yet some said it was Hendrickson himself, who talked when he was drinking.

The townsmen didn't like him, rumors aside. Some in the community wondered why a man of Mike Garrett's importance in civic affairs would associate with a fellow like Hendrickson. There was no doubt as to the man's extortion racket in the red-light district. It couldn't be proved, because the girls were afraid to talk. Several had already been beaten. Sike himself let it be known he was boss of the district.

Sike, of course, never let on that Garrett was the mastermind behind his operation. That is, he hadn't yet. But there might come a time when just such an ace up the sleeve would be nice to have. Hendrickson trusted Garrett only insofar as he had something on him. Sike believed greatly in self-protection.

What it was with Sike, most agreed, was that he was simply unpleasant. His arrogant manner, hatchet face, and brutal fists were enough to alienate him in any community. Even his cronies, of whom there were few, didn't like him. Their association was based on fear.

When he entered the office, he knew at a glance what Garrett was planning. He could tell by the big man's hot eye, the way he paced, hands behind his back, body hunched forward slightly, as though walking were a problem.

"What, boss?" he asked.

"I didn't say anything, Sike."

"You said plenty."

Garrett appraised the man from under thick eyebrows. Sike knew him much too well indeed, but he said, "Yes, I do have a problem."

"Can you tell me?"

His boss's attention swung to Molly. Seated at the typewriter, swiftly changing her employer's crabbed handwriting into print, her back was curved tightly against her dress. The sight excited Garrett. It always had. There was something about Molly that provoked the sensual in him. She wasn't exactly pretty, but she was more than that. There was more grace in the girl's most awkward movements than in, say, Ruth's entire body. Molly was fluid, strong, with an undercurrent of sexuality that inflamed him, but she'd never given him a glance. It was always "Yes, Mr. Garrett, No, Mr. Garrett"—strictly business. When he tried to be extra nice, she withdrew into a stoical silence. But she remained enticing, tantalizing, and inflammatory.

Sike, noticing where his captain's eyes were, crudely asked, "Do you want her?"

Molly stiffened, but kept typing.

"Why, what do you mean, Sike?"

"She's one fine-looking squaw."

"Yes, she is. And do you know something?"

"What, boss?"

"She likes our old friend Meeky."

"Can't trust a squaw, ever."

"Molly," said Garrett, and his voice was silky, "you do like me, don't you?"

The girl turned slowly and nodded.

"Speak up, you!" hissed Sike.

"No, no! Sike," Garrett waved a hand. "Don't be that way. She's a good Indian. If she doesn't like me, that's her business. Of course, she might lose her job . . ."

Molly's face remained the same, showing no emotion, but her heart was gripped by a sudden fear.

"What you want from me?" she asked. "Don't I do good job?"

"Oh, yes! Very good." Garrett winked at his cold-eyed lieutenant. "But, Molly, there's more to life than work. Do you know what I mean?"

Molly knew exactly what he meant, but she said "No."

Garrett laughed softly and placed a hand on her thigh.

"Oh, come on now," he said lightly, "you're from the river. Don't tell me you Indians don't know all about it by the time you're ten."

"Take your hand from me."

Sike moved to the door and locked it, his malicious face taut.

"Molly," continued Garrett smoothly, "be nice to me and my friend here, and you'll go far in the world."

"You got her."

"Her? You mean *Miss Claxton?*" Garrett hissed contemptuously. He shook his head. "No, I'm sorry to say that I don't have her. We aren't married, you see."

"You will soon."

"But I want you now, girl."

Molly squared her shoulders, defensive now, alert to bad trouble.

"Hey," husked Sike, "she wants to give a fight. That's good. I like my women feisty. More bounce, you know?"

Garrett rose, and Sike was immediately at his side. Molly stood up to meet the threat.

"You come closer," she warned, "and I holler."

"Go ahead," snarled Hendrickson. "If they hear you, so what? They don't ever come to our office. They know better."

Molly struck. The blow glanced off Sike's nose, raising a welt. Hissing like an enraged wolverine, Sike swung from the floor. His fist caught Molly on the side of her face, and she tumbled backward. He was on her at once, a rat clawing. Molly tried to scream, but he struck her again.

"I not give in to you," Molly gasped. "Honor live in me. I don't give to man I don't want."

Sike grunted. "Well, you will this time, little siwash, like me or not." He struck again, a savage blow. "You are not only having one of us, but two."

Garrett moved around to Molly's face and with his two hands squeezed her mouth shut.

"I told you to be nice," he whispered, "but you wouldn't listen."

CHAPTER 19

There was a queer silence in the office, as if all sound had been sucked out. The world was far away for Molly. She saw Garrett and Hendrickson, but they seemed at the end of a long tunnel. Garrett was speaking, but she heard nothing. His lips moved, and the bowie-knife moustache dipped and bobbed, but she didn't hear a word.

She was numb to everything except a shocked knowing of what had happened. It filled her mind with horror, and nothing else registered. Nothing else entered Molly's mind, not Garrett's voice, not Hendrickson grinning over his boss's shoulder.

Suddenly she wailed, a long, thin cry of despair.

"Shut up!" snapped Garrett, slapping her. "No more of that, or my friend will take care of you, understand?"

Molly quieted, not because of Garrett's order, because she still couldn't hear a word. But her grief went inside, sinking deeply into her being, where it would remain. She would never be totally free of what had happened to her that day. The black moustache making motions on its ruddy field of skin might as well have saved its energy. She heard nothing.

"You tell anybody about this," its owner was saying, "and there will be one less squaw in the Tanana Valley."

"Maybe I ought to dump her in the Chena," suggested Hendrickson, his pale eyes brightening.

Garrett growled a negative.

"That won't be necessary. Even if she told, who would believe her? Me, the mayor, supporter of good causes, having an Indian girl? Against her wishes?" He laughed harshly. "I got a

woman already, pretty Miss Ruth Claxton. Everybody knows
we are deeply in love. Besides"—the moustache twisted into a
leer—"I might want some of that again."

"Agreed!" came the response from Sike, who added, "You
were saying something about Claxton, boss . . ." His dog's
eyes shone with a peculiar light.

Garrett opened the door without another look at Molly.

"Let's get out of here," he said. "Little squaw doesn't want
to hear things she shouldn't."

The two left, and with their departure Molly's senses began
the journey back. She heard their booted feet on the stairway
and a series of hoarse giggles. Then they were gone.

She was lying on her back. Painfully, she straightened up and
stood swaying in the middle of the floor. She smoothed out her
dress, but her mind was closed tight, actions automatic. She put
on her coat and overshoes. Then, with averted face, she departed by the rear door, the same that Tim had fled through the
year before.

In Molly's mind were two panels of thought. One, she knew
what had happened, and, two, she knew what had to be done
about it. She had been used like an animal. She had been
beaten. Her honor was gone, her pride crushed. And the ones
who had done this to her had departed *laughing*.

Rage slowly ate away the humiliation and pain. She was
strong, and the beating left no residual effects. She never gave
second thoughts to her blackened eyes or the cut cheeks, the
split lips. But her mind burned brightly with a clear vision of
what must be done next.

The vicious acts committed against her body were a matter
of reprisal in her tribe. No man took a woman unless she allowed it. If there were a child from such a coupling, the babe
would have an evil spirit. A woman lay with a man out of respect and love, for then the child would be of good spirit, an
asset to the tribe.

Molly shuddered. If there came to be a child in her womb as a result of rape, she would kill herself before it was born.

She ran quickly through the back streets of town, aiming for Ruth Claxton's house. There was no man to avenge what had happened, but Molly's thinking had crystallized. She knew what must be done: Garrett and Hendrickson would die. Even if there was no man to avenge her, she was not afraid. She was Dihai Kutchin. *Dihai!* It was Dihai who had driven invading Inupiat Eskimos back to their arctic flatlands, north of the mountains. Dihai, the fearless, the most respected of Athabascan Indians.

Dihai Kutchin! Molly had no man to avenge her, but vengeance would be hers. She would see to it, or her honor would be forever lost! She would die for that honor.

On reaching Ruth's place, Molly reconnoitered. The house was vacant, so she entered by the back door, going directly to the bedroom. In a stand she found a pearl-handled .32-caliber revolver. It was loaded and ready. Ruth had made it a point to show her the weapon. It was Molly's conviction that Ruth feared her. Showing Molly the gun was a badly disguised warning to be good. She needn't have worried. Molly didn't like her. The lovely eyes lied. A man who fell for those eyes would land in a pit of rotted moose guts.

Tucking the pistol in a coat pocket, Molly left the bedroom, but paused by the rolltop desk. She knew about the record book, because she had worked on it. The white people thought she was too stupid to figure out why she was brought to Ruth's house to work, instead of the book being brought to her. Matter of convenience, Garrett had said, though Molly had the distinct feeling Ruth was against her seeing the book at all. Molly had said nothing. She couldn't have cared less what white people did to each other. What had that to do with her? All she wanted was to work and get paid.

Before she could roll the top back, a noise at the front of the house startled her, and she fled through the back door. Without pausing to see who or what had made the noise—it didn't matter—Molly sped toward the Aurora Tavern. Ah-saaaa! She clutched the revolver fiercely. Justice!

She let herself into the office and hid in a shadowed corner. Sooner or later, the ones who had brought disgrace to her would show up. With luck, they would be together, but maybe only one. Either way, she meant to kill them both. She would track down the remaining one if necessary. Checking the revolver's cylinder, Molly saw five cartridges. The hammer rested on an empty chamber. Five were plenty. Two would be enough!

The minutes ticked past. They dragged as the beaver drags his tail across deep snow, slowly, slowly. Each new sound from the barroom set her on edge. Garrett? Dog Eyes? The minutes bunched up into hours, and Molly was numb with waiting. Her wounds began throbbing, and her mind became a blur with too much thinking, too much tension, too much grief.

When steps did ascend the stairway, it had been so long a wait that the fact registered slowly. When it did, Molly found her hands shaking. But she raised the revolver and cocked the hammer. Whoever entered first would be shot first.

The door swung open, and Hendrickson stepped across the threshold. Molly knew well the value of correct shooting. She had intended to squeeze the trigger, but ragged nerves betrayed her and she jerked. The pistol roared with full intent, but the slug harmlessly gouged a hole in the wall.

Sike stumbled back with a screech, but he was a man who had lived through such experiences before. His reaction was instant, and from confusion to exact assessment of the situation took only a split second. He leaped on Molly, just as she triggered her next shot. Again, the bullet passed harmlessly into the wall. The two grappled for possession of the weapon. Molly was as strong as many men, but she was no match for the lean sinews of Hendrickson. His grip was iron-hard. He jerked the revolver free, then hit Molly with as much force as he could muster in an off-balance stance. She wavered, but remained on her feet.

There was an excited clamor outside the office, as customers crowded the landing to see what it was all about. Molly dashed past Hendrickson into the throng.

Hands grabbed for her, strong hands belonging to miners, trappers, and frontiersmen, hands that knew what a grip was. For a moment, Molly thought that it was all over for her. But there was one pair of hands belonging to a man with a red beard that pushed the others loose without seeming to.

"Beat it," he urged in a whisper, "I'll do what I can here."

In the confusion, nobody seemed to know exactly what he was hanging on to. Somehow most found their hands attached to the red-bearded fellow instead of the girl, while the rest saw their hands latching on to thin air.

In the meantime, Molly reached the front door and fled down the street. She crossed the Chena River bridge in giant strides and raced into the wilderness beyond.

Hendrickson hollered a posse into action and gave an earnest, deadly pursuit. But Molly hid in the brush. She heard him swearing and shouting orders. She caught a glimpse of his face once, and shivered. The dog eyes flamed with a blue light so intense that there was no mistaking their owner's wish. Molly knew that if their eyes met, hers would meet death the instant after.

But he didn't see her. Molly knew the ways of the wilderness better than any man in the posse. She left no give-away signs. Her tracks would never be seen, not even by the keenest trapper. And she was quiet, so still that a red squirrel, confused by the sudden bedlam in his country, passed within two feet of the huddled human without turning a whisker. Molly had sat thus many times in the shallow muskrat canoes of her people, waiting. If she moved, she might not eat that night.

Her pursuers searched until dark but gave up when the stars winked on. They all returned quietly, wanting a drink—all, that is, except for Sike. He pounded past Molly cursing to himself, his face a study in thwarted murder.

As his horse thundered into the distance, Molly breathed easier. She had fooled the posse, but then, white men were easy to fool. She now had a real adversary, and that was nature. She dared not go back to town. The Palace Bathhouse would be watched, as both Sike and Garrett knew she lived there. She knew nobody in town well enough to ask for help. Molly Jack was on her own.

She glanced at the sky and found it very clear. Since it was September, a clear sky meant frosts. Ponds had already been touched with ice. She had only her summer coat and light overshoes meant for rain. They were not enough. As tough as she was, as hardened to living with little in the lowest temperatures, there had always been a fire when needed, and there had always been warm clothing. Even the Dihai slowed down when the blood ran cold.

In spite of all the negatives, she took the only option left without further question. She turned north. It was well over a hundred miles to where he lived, the man-who-fought-bears. But Molly didn't think in terms of mileage. She only knew this: if she walked the Indian walk steadily, without sleep, she would reach his place in two and a half, maybe three days. There would be no stopping at a roadhouse for warmth or food—that would be like yelling to Sike, "Here I am!"

There was a trick to making time on the trail that her father had taught her. She called it the "Indian walk": run a ways, then walk a ways, then run again. Do this without stopping, and the miles would go behind.

She set her broad face northward, deciding to run first, then walk. Though she knew her situation was like that of two dogs stuck back to back, she was not afraid. In town she was afraid; in the wilderness she was home again.

As she ran, she remembered there was somebody to whom she owed much, a white man at that. Who was he in the red beard?

CHAPTER 20

Tim elbowed his way through a sea of willows and alder. There was nothing so resistant to mankind, he was certain, as a thick tangle of Alaskan brush. You were damned lucky to get through even a small patch without tripping flat on your face.

He ducked his head into the massed resistance and plunged on, his daily hike about over.

Ever since he'd fought Jake, he had been confused. To get away from his thoughts and yet, paradoxically, to bring them to order, he had been walking a lot. He'd beat on his best friend without a second's hesitation. Jake had done nothing except aim at a wolf who was hurting his business. The man had every right, but he, Timothy Meeker, had stopped him with his fists.

What did it take for him to stand up to Garrett and that ominous shadow, Hendrickson? He went hot and cold when it came to that pair. And they really needed cutting down to size, to put the matter mildly.

Tim sighed and plowed ahead. Was he really a user, as Jake said? Certainly there was every indication of it. He had gone over the matter a dozen times since Jake's accusation. He had finally ceased blushing with mortification, though the idea still caused considerable embarrassment. He had never wanted to hide behind anybody. How little he knew himself.

But if Tim would concede that Jake had been correct in his diagnosis to a point, he wouldn't agree one hundred percent. True, he had used Garrett, and, yes, all of them, to some degree, but he had also called on the rights of friendship. This was especially true of Jake and Riley. He would have done the same for them, had their lives been turned upside down. As for Garrett, he had used him, he could see that now. He'd known Mike was a crook, as Jake pointed out, but he kept right on partnering with the man. That was usage, pure and simple. He had liked the money Garrett was bringing in—all of it, the bad and the good.

Tim took out his pipe and lit up. The sun was under the western mountains, and a few of the brighter stars had turned on. Street lights of the universe, thought Tim, though they wouldn't do much good. Starlight never brightened old Earth that much. You needed a good moon.

He stepped up his pace, having no desire to crash around after dark. There was no danger of getting lost, with Birch Creek as guide, but brush pounding at night was a nuisance.

In the quickening dusk, he approached a cow moose and her five-month calf. Like a shadow, she floated away, the calf at her side. Neither made the slightest sound, and Tim marveled. Moose, the most ungainly and largest of the deer family, seemed to roam the forests on elevated hoofs. As he drew abreast, the cow gave a warning grumble, and her hackles went up.

"Don't get your nose in a knot, sis," Tim assured the glaring mother. "I'm not interested in your child."

"Baah!" grunted the anxious parent, having the last word, as Tim struggled out of sight.

Night dropped swiftly, once it started, and he was forced to grope.

"I never learn," he growled to the distant stars. "I've been hiking since I was five, and still haven't enough sense to hit the back trail home in time."

In spite of his dissatisfaction, he arrived at the cabin fifteen minutes later. It was a welcome sight except for one thing: there was a light in the window. No lamp had been burning when he left. You never left a lamp burning in an empty cabin.

Somebody was in the house.

Carrying his rifle at the ready, he ran to a side window and peeked in. A woman sat in a chair, facing the stove, her back to him. But Tim knew that back, and he recognized the long, dark hair. Molly Jack was waiting.

Knocking once to give notice, he entered. Molly whirled, and he stopped dead, shocked by the torn features that greeted him.

Both of the girl's eyes were blackened. Her lips were split and swollen, and there were blue-green bruises covering her cheeks. Her nose had been cut, and raw flesh showed red in the deep wounds. There was a ring of bruises around her neck, too, as if she'd been gripped by fingers of iron.

"Molly!" he exclaimed, horrified. "What . . . ?"

"And that not all, what you see," Molly's voice was tight with exhaustion, "I got more all over me."

"What happened?" Tim was so shaken he could hardly find his tongue. "Why aren't you in town?" he finished, feeling inane when the question popped out. Obviously, there was good reason.

She didn't meet his eyes.

"How did you know I was here? I never told you about this place!"

"I stop at Riley's," said the girl. "He tell me."

"Why didn't you stay in Central?"

"No," the girl's lips formed a stubborn line, "I come to see you. Riley, he give me coffee and bread, but I don't stay there. Maybe I make mistake coming here. You have no reason to like Molly."

"Because you told Garrett I was in town? I don't hold that against you, you know that, or you wouldn't be here."

She looked at him from a darkness more engulfing than the deepest night, and she began to cry. He took her to him gently.

"Hey," he said, "you don't have to cry here. I am your friend." He thought about what he had said, and added, "I am more than your friend, girl. Much more than that."

But the sobs went on, a releasing of hurt to both body and

spirit, a response to kindness that overwhelmed her. For a moment, Molly was a child again, with no womanly inhibition, no pride to forbid tears.

Tim brought her closer to him and loved the dear body shivering against his own. She was a young girl, after all, who needed comfort for something grisly and horrible that had savaged her spirit.

He stroked the long hair and said nothing, allowing the grief to run its course. When she quieted, he led her to the bunk. She sat down, and he wrapped a blanket around her shoulders. Then he stirred the fire and started coffee. Molly watched with haunted eyes, but relief was showing through the pain, the relief of an abandoned and frightened soul finding safe harbor.

Neither spoke, Tim sensing that the Indian girl wished to go slow, sorting her thoughts, as he himself had so recently done.

When the coffee was boiled to the proper steaming black, he filled two mugs and added a little whiskey to each.

"Drink this," he directed, handing a mug to the girl. "The whiskey isn't enough to make you drunk. It will help."

Molly received the cup gratefully and sipped. She made a face, but sipped again and smiled approvingly. She held on to her silence, though, and Tim's curiosity politely maintained its distance. What had happened? The last time he'd seen her, she was the competent office clerk, doing her job. But now?

When at length she did speak, Molly's voice was heavy with irony.

"And I think," she said, "that education, that will make me different."

"But you were doing well," said Tim, "though I could have wished a better employer for you."

To this, Molly nodded violently, then subsided into the safe grounds of silence. She stared moodily at her feet.

Tim followed her gaze and received the second shock of the night. He had noticed only the powerful story of her face until now, when he saw her feet. Her boots were ripped and lay open, exposing bloody flesh. Her coat was ragged and hung like a sack. It was speckled with spruce needles and smears of dirt. Those clothes had been through much more than they were meant for.

Tim was suddenly aware of what had happened. "Molly, did you walk from town?"

She nodded.

"My God! Why? You could have frozen out there!"

Some of the old spirit flashed.

"No! Indian can take care of himself!"

"Indians are flesh and blood just like whites," insisted Tim.

"I not frozen, am I?" The question, meant to come out triumphantly, was barely a whisper.

"No."

Another suspicion was forming in Tim's brain.

"Have you eaten in the past several days?"

"Only a little at Riley's." She emptied her mug and held it out for more. "I hungry."

Tim poured the coffee but left the whiskey out. "No sleep?"

"I rest a little."

"Are you going to tell me what happened?"

"I say yes, but not yet. Maybe I make a mistake coming here."

"Well," Tim returned agreeably, "I won't know about that until you tell me, will I!"

"I starved."

Tim got a candle and went to the cache. Lighting the candle, he stuck it to a little shelf, then lifted a moose loin to a plank table. The meat was frozen an inch down, but it sliced easily under his sheath knife.

Meat wasn't uppermost in his mind. Molly was. She had come to him because she was in trouble. Man trouble, maybe? Drinking? She'd left town abruptly, that was obvious from her clothes. They were definitely not for the trail. And why hadn't she stopped at the roadhouses?

When he returned with two thick steaks, she was setting water buckets on the stove.

"I am dirty," she said, "from long trip, and other things."

"Other things?"

Molly flicked him a look, but ventured nothing.

"Molly! What happened?"

"I eat and take bath first."

Tim looped a blanket over a drying line strung across the room. He carried a galvanized tub in and set it near the stove to warm up. Then he rummaged around in a box and found a shirt and trousers.

"Wear these," he offered, tossing them to Molly. "They won't fit, but they are clean."

He got his first-aid kit, and when the water warmed, he bathed her wounds in a boric acid solution. They didn't look dangerous, though assuredly painful enough.

Molly sat perfectly still while he gently cleansed her face and feet, sat like a little girl who loved the feel of caring hands.

When he had finished, she said, "I cook the meal, you wait. Read or something."

"I can cook."

"No. I think I do better. Woman cook. You sit." She pushed him to a chair and thrust a book into his hands. "Read!"

The volume was one of Jake's Shakespeare set, and Tim was in no way up to the nuances of sixteenth-century writing just then. His mind was alive with questions, but tact regulated his tongue. When Molly was ready, she would talk. He had a drink, but she declined. When the meal was ready, she told him, "Sit!"

The steaks were excellent, and Tim admitted they were a hell of a lot better than he could have done. Along with fried potatoes and canned peas, it was a banquet, but he was too distracted to enjoy the meal as much as it deserved. His heart went out to the girl when she carefully tucked the food between swollen lips.

"God!" he exploded. "Who did this to you?"

Molly gripped her fork tightly, but said nothing.

"You mean you actually walked through that wilderness without stopping anyplace?"

Tim still had a hard time believing.

"Why stop?" countered the girl. "I have no money. And, anyway," her voice dropped, "who want a squaw in their place?"

"Stop that talk!" snapped Tim. "You are as good as any woman."

"I look like this, and everybody scared."

Tim had to admit that she was right. Her face was a raw, swollen horror. But he knew he wasn't getting a complete answer, either.

Molly interrupted his growing insistence by picking up her steak in her fingers.

"Godmen, they say this not nice," she mumbled with a full mouth, "but it's fast."

After the meal, the bath water was hot, and she slipped behind the blanket. Seconds later, Tim heard splashing. Such intimacy with another human pleased him. It turned the cabin into a—home. He also noted that Molly seemed to trust him, in spite of what his intentions had once been.

"You need more water?" he called and was informed "Lots."

Tim filled the buckets from a large barrel next to the stove and set them on to heat. He stoked the fire, glad for the hot-burning birch he had cut. The water warmed quickly.

"Want me to pour?"

"No!" There was a hint of amusement in the negative, the first signs of relaxing Tim had noticed. "Molly's strong. She pour."

"Just asking."

When the bath was over, the girl stepped into view dressed in

Tim's clothing. It hung from her but she hugged herself, pleased.

"I feel good now," she said, then scowled. "Not like before." Her face flattened into a barren landscape, as she remembered. "I don't even know it was real. It seems like a bad dream, you know? I wake up soon, and it all go away."

"Are you going to tell me what happened?" Tim was exasperated with waiting.

"I empty water first" was the reply.

"We'll both do it."

Each took a handle of the tub and together they carried it outdoors. After it was emptied, Tim hung it from a nail on the cabin wall. Then they returned to the snugness inside.

"You're strong," observed Tim.

"Indian woman, she have to be strong to fight . . ." She broke off and turned to the stove.

Tim took her shoulders and turned her back to him.

"Molly," he said quietly so as not to agitate the situation needlessly, "if you tell me what happened, maybe you'll feel better."

"You don't like me after I tell. No man will like me again, not ever!" There was so much rage and grief in Molly's outburst that Tim stood back. "I hate those mens for this. I hate you white men!"

"Do you hate me?"

"No! Oh, no! I don't talk right. It's crazy."

Tim poured more coffee, taking his time, waiting. He lit his pipe. Molly, meanwhile, quieted, but her face was a stern portrait in unhappiness. Whatever had happened, thought Tim, was bad. The worst.

"It was Garrett and that terrible one," Molly nearly shouted, "him with the ice eyes!"

Tim felt a chill. "Hendrickson? Why did he beat you?"

Molly's broken face twisted in an agony of indecision.

"Tell me!" ordered Tim. "I've got to know. Both of them

beat you up, didn't they? Why?—did you find out about their crooked deals?"

"Not that, but I know something there, too."

"What then." Tim leaned forward. "What!"

Molly was quiet another moment, then she sighed and said in a low voice, "They have me, those men." She stopped, then added, "I mean the crazy-eye one, he have me, and I don't want that. I fight, and he beat me."

The enormity of what Molly was telling him took a few seconds to register. Tim shivered, a reaction to the heat of a great anger starting to boil in his gut. His cheeks grew hot with a blood-flush of fury.

"You mean that son of a bitch raped and beat you?"

"Yes." Molly met his gaze at last. "And Garrett, him, too."

"*Garrett!*"

Molly looked into the bleak eyes facing her. "Yes, Garrett. And I know where he keeps record of bad things. I think you want that."

Blacktail howled outside, a long, beautiful roll of music in the hills, but for the first time Tim didn't hear him.

CHAPTER 21

With the abrupt disappearance of Molly, Garrett was forced to some abrupt thinking. Her disappearance meant his control was slipping. He hadn't expected such a reaction from an Indian. Molly was not the first native girl he'd taken by force. It was conceivable she would not be his last. But she was the first to attempt vengeance, which meant he'd misjudged her. Perhaps he should have listened to Sike's advice, after all. The Chena Slough solved a lot of headaches. With the girl out of sight, she also became a threat. Oh! not much of a threat, but she could become a nuisance. More than a nuisance, perhaps. She could holler rape at a time, for example, when he was on the public trail to high office. Garrett was savvy enough politically to realize that even if he convinced the populace that he had never raped anybody, the stigma would remain. And that could be damaging.

Molly Jack would have to be killed. No other insurance measured up.

The big man's bowie-knife moustache was stiff as a file, indicating great displeasure in its owner. Damn it! What had come over him, anyway? Sike—he was to blame. If Sike hadn't put the idea into his head, nothing would have happened. Not then, anyway. There was a time and place for everything, and the office hadn't been it. Not for the Indian girl, anyway.

No, he'd made a serious error, and he knew it. The man who led him into this sticky morass would pay, but not yet. Sike was still needed. There was Ruth to take care of first.

He had been working toward that end for some time, and his

scheme was going well. He and Ruth had been seen everywhere together. He had made it a point to be at Ruth's side, arm in arm, as it were, very much in love. The newspapers carried stories about the two of them planning for the future. A detailed accounting of their dream house, now under construction, was published weekly. It was a sort of "young love" thing that appealed to folks of all ages. Voter bait.

Ruth was flattered by his increased attention and only yesterday had said, "I thought you were seeing other women."

That jolted Garrett, and he blurted, "What do you mean?"

"Well, nothing, really. Just chatter." The beautiful eyes narrowed. "Michael, have you been seeing other women?"

"No, of course not!"

"You mean I'm your true love?" There was more than a trace of acid in the well modulated words.

"I swear it," replied Garrett, while mentally kicking himself for nearly tipping his hand.

"I haven't seen Molly around," continued Ruth mercilessly. "Where is she, Mike?"

"I had to fire her. Got lippy. You know how squaws are. Give 'em a little work, and they own you."

That had ended the conversation, but later Mike thought it over. You never could tell about Ruth Claxton. She was sly. What did she know about the Jack girl? Maybe nothing, and maybe she'd been listening at the door. Damn that Sike!

It was time to get things going. By now, the whole country thought he was madly in love with Ruth. Perhaps Ruth didn't think that, but, then, it didn't matter what she thought, did it? The last person in the world the authorities would suspect after Ruth vanished would be Mike Garrett, courtly swain.

On Saturday evening, five days after Molly's disappearance, Garrett had a short conversation with Hendrickson.

"It will be tonight," he said.

Sike's dog eyes glistened.

"What time?" he asked.

"Make it late. We want to be sure there will be nobody to see us. Meet me here after the bar closes."

Sike grinned, and Garrett noted how like a curved snake his lips were.

"And"—Hendrickson's voice was soft—"you know what I was promised."

Garrett shrugged.

"I don't care what you do with the woman before you Chena-ize her," he snickered at his play on words. "Just do it silently."

"Some things are best in private, boss."

"You weren't so private the other day."

"Injuns is different."

And all because of one of them, thought Garrett, while smiling like the July sun, your time is short, bucko.

The hours passed slowly for Mike Garrett. He was under more pressure than he liked to admit. Thank God it would be over soon.

The hour finally did arrive. Garrett waited for half an hour to make sure the drunks were off the streets, then he and Sike walked quickly to Ruth's house. It was just past two-thirty in the morning.

Garrett had a key, but the door was unlocked. Burglary was nonexistent in Fairbanks, doors seldom locked. The two entered stealthily, cats stalking a bird. Once inside, they made no pretense and stamped to the bedroom, Garrett having reason to know where it was.

Ruth, aroused by the commotion, sat up in bed, exclaiming, "Mike! What . . . !"

Then she saw Hendrickson over Garrett's shoulder. There was a tension in the man's hatchet face that told much. Ruth knew she was in immediate danger. She reached for her revolver in the bedside stand and found—nothing. She stared at the empty drawer in disbelief.

"Can't find your little protector?" Garrett asked pleasantly. "Somebody must have taken it."

"You did!" exclaimed Ruth, her nerves rigid with a terrible premonition.

"The Indian girl," Sike put in. "I got your gun from her."

"Why would she have it?" asked Ruth, growing more alarmed.

"She was robbing the office," said Hendrickson, his snake lips curved in a wide sinister grin.

Garrett interrupted with, "All this talk is unnecessary. Let's finish our business."

Ruth huddled under the covers. She knew perfectly well what Garrett's use of the word "business" meant. It could be interchanged, insofar as she was concerned, with "dead."

"You are going to kill me," she said faintly. "Why, Mike?"

"Good insurance, Ruth," purred Garrett, happy with the way things were going. "I'm sure you know what I mean, darling girl. Dead lips are silent lips. I do unto you, before you do unto me."

"Mike, I swear! I had nothing of the sort in mind. I love you!"

"I can read the signs, sweetheart," was the curt reply. "Now, then"—his voice hardened—"let me have the key to your desk."

"I don't know where it is."

"That's dumb. Give it to me, quick."

Sike stepped forward with upraised fist. Ruth hastily dug in the drawer where the gun had been and handed Garrett a key.

Mike smiled his satisfaction and turned to leave, saying to Hendrickson, "Have fun, but hurry. We don't have much time."

"Mike!" screamed Ruth. "For God's sake, don't leave me with him!"

Garrett turned, blew her a kiss, and then shut the door behind him with a sharp click. He listened intently. There was a dull fleshy thud, as of a fist connecting. He heard Ruth gasp, then there were sounds of a struggle.

He left the door and unlocked the desk. The familiar book was easy to locate, and Garrett sighed with relief. In it lay enough evidence to damn him forever. With Ruth's disappearance, the law would be sure to search the house thoroughly, but they'd never find that book! Just as dead women told no tales, neither did, ah, Chena-ized records.

From the bedroom issued muffled cries, the pleadings of Ruth, mingled with Sike's whinny-like giggles, and the thud of fists. Garrett cocked his head, the better to listen.

A gale-force storm on what Tim knew as Twelve Mile Summit drove snow in stinging lines across the world. Tim buried his face deep in the sheepskin collar of his mackinaw and urged Buck on. He reached over to clear packed ice crystals from the horse's muzzle.

Ahead, dim in the battering wind, was Molly. She sat a steed borrowed from Riley, and she was dressed to withstand the evils of fall travel. Had the storm caught her three days before, she would have died.

The ground was not frozen yet, and the snow didn't stick. Instead, it melted on contact, turning the trail into a furrow of mud, slowing progress.

Tim cursed, but maintained his patience. They were going as fast as conditions permitted. Once off the summit, the snow should, he hoped, lessen. They still had ninety miles to go, and he wanted to cover that in two days—or less.

The decision to go after Garrett and Hendrickson had been immediate. Tim was so filled with disgust and rage, he would have walked to Fairbanks barefooted. After all, Molly had done practically that in her worthless boots.

When she realized how deep Tim's anger went, Molly was frightened.

"I don't come out here for you to revenge me," she said anxiously. "I only come because I have nowhere else to go."

"I know," replied Tim, "but this thing is beyond you now, Molly. There's nothing you can do about how I feel."

"You get hurt," she protested, "and I don't want that."

"Garrett is going to get hurt" was the response. "Not me. And that killer Hendrickson. They have to be exposed for what they are."

Tim banged a fist into his open hand. "Damn it! Maybe this wouldn't have happened if I'd acted like a man long ago, Molly. If I'd have fought Garrett when I first knew he was crooked . . . Damn me! I'm a weak man, Molly!"

"You not weak."

"Those two birds have flown high long enough," ranted Tim. "Would you want the next governor of Alaska to be an extortionist? A cheat—a rapist?"

"I don't care who is chief in white man's country. No business of mine. I don't want you to get hurt is all."

"It's time I got hurt!" exploded Tim, with a vehemence that surprised even him. "Only it's not going to happen that way."

In a last-ditch measure, Molly pointed out, "It's September month. The high places, they will catch us in storm, maybe. No good. We freeze."

For an answer, Tim dug out heavy clothing.

"Wear these," he said, "and no more argument. We are leaving."

Molly knew she was licked, but she was stubborn.

"You don't need to hurry," she claimed. "I think they be in there a long time."

"Yeah, tearing apart the lives of others." Tim's jaw tightened. "Listen, I *can't* wait. I've waited too long already. I've excused a lot of things in Garrett because I was stupid. But he and that dog-eyed bastard he chums with aren't going to hurt people I love. Do you understand?"

Molly's eyes widened.

"Yes!" roared Tim. "I love you! You sleep on the bed, I'll take the floor, and we leave early in the morning."

As he hoped, the storm slackened its intensity, when they dropped down the south slope of the summit. He picked a camping spot next to a stream he called Faith Creek, though Molly couldn't have cared less what he called it, she was so weary. They were still about eighty miles from town.

"Damn it!" swore Tim. "Why does this country have to be so big!"

They'd brought two sleeping bags, one for each. Even with such preparations, Tim was reluctant to spend any time using them. As far as he was concerned, he'd have pushed through with only the briefest rest periods. But he acknowledged that Molly was already worn fine from her outbound struggle. And horses were, after all, horseflesh. They needed a break.

He started a fire in a stand of stunted spruce trees. When it was crackling, Molly scraped a few embers aside for a cooking blaze. She had fried potatoes, bacon, and coffee ready by the time Tim unsaddled and hobbled the horses.

Though their elevation was still high, near the headwaters of the Chatanika River, the first snow had come and gone. The second snow, with more permanent intentions, was waiting the chime of the seasonal clock. Tim reckoned that would be the storm they had passed through earlier. Chances were it would settle a deep fall in the valley by the next evening. He and Molly had been smart to leave when they did. After the first permanent snow with its blowing drifts, the trail was blocked for several days, until freighters plowed through with sleds.

They had finished eating, and Tim had just lit his pipe, when Molly said, "That man, he helped me."

"What man helped you where?"

"You know, when I hit Dog Eyes and run, the man was in the people I run through. He have a red beard, and say something like 'You go quick, and I hold them back.' It give me time to get away, I think."

Mickey Jenderson, of course! Tim made a mental note to thank that man with all the thanks he could give.

"I know him," he said. "He's a friend. He knew you from what I told him."

He wondered whether Sike had caught on. If so, Mickey was dead. All the more reason to get to town quickly. Tim groaned. God, what rotten weather and the need for rest was doing to him. While he sat on his ass, maybe that hatchet-faced killer was drawing a bead on a real man.

The next morning, they were on the trail at daybreak. The horses, rested, were eager, and Tim moved Buck along swiftly. His sense of urgency had increased on waking, and he pushed hard. Molly led as before, but the pace was set by Tim and Buck.

They made good time that day, pausing at a point twenty miles from town. It was ten in the evening.

"Let's stay," begged Molly, whose face was ashen with fatigue. "I so tired."

But Tim was adamant.

"We're too close now," he said. "We'll have to finish tonight. I could never camp here, knowing those two were so close."

He leaned over and kissed Molly. "Let's go. There will be plenty of time to rest later."

As they pushed the tired horses on, Tim checked the .30-30 carbine that Riley had loaned him. It was loaded and ready.

At a little after two-thirty, they crossed the Chena Slough into town. The streets were empty and a hasty consultation was held.

"Let's get Garrett right now," said Tim. "I can't wait to see his eyes when he gazes down this gun barrel." He patted the .30-30.

"Yes, but I think it is good to have that book, too," suggested Molly. "Maybe get it first, so nothing will happen to it, you know?"

"Smart thinking, girl." Tim leaned from Buck and kissed her again. "Let's go."

CHAPTER 22

As they neared Ruth's house, Molly held up her hand and dismounted.

"I think we go on foot from here. Horses, they make noise."

They slipped up on the place from the rear, and were surprised to hear noises from inside. A man was swearing brutally, to the accompaniment of feminine screams.

"Something is happening," whispered Molly. "That noise, it comes from bedroom."

The two entered through the rear door and passed through a darkened kitchen to the living room. Garrett, in lamplight, stood in the center, head slanted, listening. The bowie-knife moustache was pointed at a steep angle upward, signifying his enjoyment. He clenched the vital book in a white-knuckled grip.

Tim stepped into the light.

"Mike," he said, as Molly appeared beside him, "what's going on in there?"

"You!" Garrett exclaimed, gaping at the girl.

"It is me, yes," replied Molly. "You who take woman and beat her—you hope I dead, maybe?"

"See something you don't like, Garrett?" prodded Tim. "Now what in hell is going on in there?" He jabbed a thumb at the bedroom.

Garrett still made no answer, but his eyes turned crafty.

Alerted, Tim raised the carbine too late. Garrett jerked a pistol from his shoulder holster and fired in one quick motion. The .30-30 bellowed, but Tim missed.

He levered another shell into the chamber, but in the time

that took, Garrett squeezed off another shot. The slug grazed Tim's hand. He dropped the carbine and staggered back in reaction to the sting.

Mike ran into the night, still clutching the book. Tim chased him for a short distance, but gave it up. It was a fool's errand, because night served as a perfect cover for ambush. He returned to the house on the run. Mike could be dealt with later.

As he entered, Hendrickson opened the bedroom door, pistol in hand. When he saw Tim, a thin smile snaked across his face.

"Well what do you know?" he said joyfully. "I got me a Meeky!"

He raised his weapon to shoot, when his action was interrupted by the slamming voice of the .30-30. Sike jerked back a step, seeing Molly for the first time. She held the carbine ready to fire again.

"Good God!" exclaimed Hendrickson, "I've been killed by a squaw."

His words trailed off, and he sank to the floor. Bright crimson blood gushed from his mouth, and his feet drummed the carpet. He convulsed, flopped over on his back, glazing eyes fixed on Molly.

She stared in horror, as Sike lay dying.

"I knew we should have killed you," muttered Hendrickson. His head rolled back in death. Sike would cause no more problems for anybody. His raping days were over.

Molly thrust the rifle from her.

"Ah-deeee!" she exclaimed softly to Tim. "I had to shoot, he would have killed you."

Tim circled her shoulders with a comforting arm.

"You didn't shoot a man," he said, "you shot a mad animal. You saved my life."

A noise from the bedroom attracted their attention.

Ruth, face bloodied and swollen, staggered to the door.

"He was going to kill me . . ."

She buried her torn face in her hands. "Oh, my God! And

Mike was with him. He knew what was happening and didn't even try to help." She shivered at the sight of Hendrickson's limp body at her feet.

Molly went to her and took the woman in her arms. "Hey," she said soothingly, "he not do that again."

Tim had thought his feelings for Ruth were over, but at the moment, his heart was filled with pity. No matter what she was, Ruth didn't deserve what she got.

"Listen," he said to Molly, "I've got to find Garrett before he cooks up too many lies about this. I want that book." He patted Ruth's shoulder. "We'll get a doctor for you," he said kindly, "and, Molly, call the law, too. I want this all accounted for."

He turned to leave, when Ruth said, "Don't worry about the book, Tim. I have a complete duplicate."

"Good. Garrett has probably thrown his into the Chena by now. We'll talk about it later."

He ran to Buck and rushed the horse to the Aurora, leaving the sorrel a block away. He went to the office, half expecting to find Garrett, but the big man wasn't there. Not yet.

Tim was settled in a chair before he realized he had no firearms. It was too late to worry about it now. He'd have to wait and see what happened.

He allowed his eyes to rove over the room. It hadn't changed much in a year and a half. Had it been only that long? It seemed like a century. He had lived a lifetime, and a lot had happened.

For one thing, he was aware of a change in himself. He no longer felt like Timid Meeky. There was a hard core inside him that rejected the designation. A different man moved to the beat of his heart.

Where had the change taken place? When? After he fought the bear? When he built the cabin? But those happenings, as significant as they might be, were not the whole answer. Other things had contributed, such as the months in jail. Jail would change anybody. He'd come through the experience, more aware of the bad side of life. He could feel, still, the courthouse shaking as a man died on the gallows. Yes, jail had had its effect.

What about his fight with Jake? That was a turning point, no doubt about it. As Jake pointed out: it was the first time Tim had ever stood up for something he believed in. Jake had felt Tim's loyalties were misplaced, but, misplaced or not, he had fought for them. It was true. He would never allow his friend to kill Blacktail. Not as long as he breathed the fresh Alaskan air, and that brought him round-robin to the wolf.

Blacktail, he knew, had had more influence on his life over the past months than any other single cause. He loved that wolf. Even if they'd never so much as "howdied," and never would, he loved the animal. He admired the wolf's independence, his ability to survive both the firearms and traps of man and natural enemies. He loved the beautiful music that Blacktail and his kin sent through the world.

He had fought for the wolf and, in fighting, had emerged somebody else, somebody who staked boundaries and held them against intruders. That was the mark of a man.

A noise in the barroom notified him somebody was on the way. He stood up, waiting. The door swung open, and Garrett faced him.

"Hello, Mike."

"Why, Timmy, what brings you here?"

The bowie-knife moustache went up in a pleasant smile.

"You know why I'm here, Mike. Where's the book?"

"Ah," the moustache still smiled. "Well, Timid, the Chena knows. Ask the river."

"You're more rotten than I could have imagined, Mike. First, you attack a defenseless Indian girl, and now we find you listening while Dog Eyes Hendrickson goes after your fiancée. What kind of man are you?"

"Don't know what you're talking about, little chum."

"You can't lie about it, Garrett."

"Lie? What do you mean, lie?"

"There are witnesses."

"Who?"

"Molly, me, and Ruth herself."

"Oh?" Garrett laughed. "You mean that a court would believe a convict, an ignorant squaw, and a trollop against the mayor?"

"Mike, even if you threw the book away, Ruth has a duplicate. And she'll use it now. You're a goner."

Garrett's eyes narrowed at that news. He drew his pistol and said, "Caught you robbing me again, buddy. Going to have to shoot you."

The gun roared, and Tim felt a blow to his shoulder as he leaped on Mike.

The two men crashed to the floor, Tim trying to wrest the weapon from Mike. They rolled over, knocking furniture askew, hitting with their free fists. Tim gripped the pistol by the barrel, twisting it, when another cartridge exploded. Garrett stiffened and looked at Tim as if surprised. His hold on the gun relaxed, and Tim pulled it free, then he stood up. But Garrett remained on the floor, a red stain spreading over his shirt.

"Mike," said Tim, "I'm sorry this had to happen."

Garrett didn't answer. His eyes closed a moment, then opened again, fixing on Tim.

"Why, Tim Meeker," said Garrett in a clear, strong voice, "Tim Meeker, it is."

The eyes shut and remained shut this time. Garrett seemed to sink in on himself. The man with the bowie-knife moustache had spoken his last words.

As Tim gazed on the body of his one-time partner and friend, he felt no elation over his victory, only sadness. What the hell, he thought, it's crazy. It's just crazy.

He was still looking down at Mike when Molly and Tod Cowles arrived.

"Figured you'd be here," said the lawman. "Is he dead?"

"Yes, he's dead."

"How did it happen?"

Tim related events, then asked, "Does that make me a wanted man again?"

Cowles shook his head.

"I don't think so. We've been watching Garrett and Hendrickson for some time now. Red-light girls have made complaints about extortion, and some of the miners have sworn they were rolled after an evening at the Aurora. And after talking with Miss Claxton a few minutes ago, I think Garrett got off easy."

Molly bent over and touched Garrett's moustache.

"Ah-saaaa!" she whispered. "It's only hair."

Tim was confined to the hospital for two weeks with his wound. But he wasn't idle.

First he had John Clark find Mickey Jenderson. When Mickey arrived, he wore a pleased smile.

"I knew you wasn't afraid of that bastard Garrett," he said.

"That's not what I wanted to see you about," said Tim.

"What then?"

"I want you to run the Aurora for me."

Jenderson was immediately all negatives.

"Hell, I don't know anything about that kind of work, Tim. The paper shuffle would kill me. I wouldn't know how to handle it, my friend."

Tim was equally positive.

"Are you through drinking?"

"Yep."

"For good?"

"I don't change, Tim."

"All right, now listen: John Clark will handle the paper work. What I want you to do is run the card games and the bartenders. Keep them all honest. I know you can do that, Mick."

"Well, sure, yes."

"All right. It's settled. You start now."

"Now?"

"This minute."

Among the matters that had been taking place during Tim's early hospitalization was Ruth's voluntary confession to the forged bill of sale. She also turned over her copy of the damaging record book to the authorities. Since the bill of sale was now admittedly false, Tim was again full partner, with access to the Aurora's resources, including its bank accounts. Whatever else Garrett might have been, he was a good businessman, and the accounts were large.

Tim had a talk about Ruth with John Clark.

"She's confessed to the forgery," said Tim. "How does she stand with the law?"

"She might get three years."

"I want the charges dropped."

"After what she's done to you?"

Tim shrugged.

"I can afford to be generous, John."

"That's fine, but the district attorney might get her on perjury."

"Oh?"

"Don't forget: it was her testimony, in part, that sent you to jail."

There was little Tim could do about that, but he stuck to his decision to have the forgery charges dropped. He got two thousand dollars together and put the money in an envelope. After this, he asked Clark to send Ruth to see him.

Ruth arrived in the afternoon. The swelling from Sike's blows was still evident, and her lovely eyes, eyes that Tim once cherished, were haunted. Even as Molly's had been, thought Tim.

"Thanks," she said, "for dropping the charges. I'm not surprised."

"You know you still might get called on perjury?"

"Yes. It doesn't matter."

Tim handed her the envelope.

"Take this money," he said, "and leave Fairbanks when you can. There's enough to get you started someplace else."

"Oh, Tim!" she exclaimed. "I was a fool, wasn't I!"

Some of the pity that Tim felt when he saw her beaten that fateful night had remained with him.

"No," he said quietly, "you were mistaken, maybe, but not a fool."

She turned to leave, then paused by the door. "I know what I was, Tim, but thank you for being a gentleman about it."

Molly, who was with him almost constantly, was last but far from least on his mind.

"Now," he said to her, "there is just one thing left to do."

"What?"

"You and I get married."

"When we do that?"

"We'll go to Central. Jake is on his trapline, and I want him and Riley, my two good friends, to be with us."

"Yes," said Molly.

With plans to return to Fairbanks in two or three weeks, he and Molly followed the mailman across the snow-blown passes.

Their wedding was held in Riley's roadhouse, conducted by a preacher from Circle. Friends, acquaintances, and strangers were present, including Frank Leach at the Springs and Deputy Dwyer, who kept shaking his head and drinking scotch. Lindstrum, nervous in new woolen pants and shirt, proved adequate as a best man. The after-wedding party was at its height when Tim and Molly slipped away, heading for the homestead.

"No shivaree for us," whispered Tim. "I want privacy!"

That evening, with a quiet October hush in the land, Blacktail howled nearby. It was a solo—just the wolf. His song, deep and rolling, thrilled Tim, as always.

He slipped an arm around Molly's waist and said to the echoes of Blacktail's song, "Thank you, my friend. I owe you much."

And he kissed his bride, the Indian girl who had brought the biggest change of all into his life.